BLOOD OF ROSES

EDWARD IV AND TOWTON

A NOVELLA BY J.P. REEDMAN

Chapter One

December 29, 1460, Wakefield.

Mud oozed under the feet of men and horse's hooves. Blood blossomed on a thin crust of snow, sank down to mingle with the churned soil. Above, the towers of Sandal castle stood bleak against the wintry sky, dark fingers against a sky heavy with an impending new snowfall.

Richard Duke of York lay dead upon the field of battle, his lifeless body stretched out on the ground before his jeering enemies. Helmetless, his rich armour was stripped away, his hair clotted with blood and brain. Lured out from his stronghold in the belief a Christmas truce with the Lancastrians would hold, he had been eager to forage for supplies with his starving men. However, a large Lancastrian army lay hidden in the woodlands around Wakefield, that haunt of outlaws since the days of Robin Hood. Margaret Anjou's forces…waiting.

James Butler, Earl of Wiltshire, Earl of Ormonde, one of leading Lancastrian captains, slammed his bloody sword into its sheath, uncaring of its gory condition. Raising his visor, he stalked around to view York's body. Despite nearing forty, he was a handsome man, with even features, high cheekbones and near-black curling hair. He was known at court for his striking looks…but also for fleeing from the battlefields.

Today he tried not to think on mockery; today he felt he had acquitted himself well—surely, he would win high favour with Queen Margaret. Her hated foe was slain, the man who would have takes away her son's right to the throne. She would be grateful…and, hopefully, generous.

"May there be peace at last without the posturing of this disloyal miscreant." Squint-eyed, satisfied, he gazed at the corpse of the dead Duke cooling in the snow. "Long live good King Henry and Queen Margaret, and their son Prince Edward. Death to all traitors."

Leaning over York's body, he grasped the limp, bloodied hand, ripping away the battered gauntlet, which he flung aside with a noisy clang. The Duke's hands were undamaged, having been well protected by the metal of those gloves. A ring with a green stone gleamed on his finger; Butler ripped it off and tossed it at a foot soldier standing nearby, who caught it clumsily in his red-smeared hands.

"You, come." Butler nodded towards the startled man, whose face was painted in crimson stripes from the carnage. Not his own blood—but that of some dead Yorkist. "Drag this carrion to a cart, I bid you. I would not touch such foulness."

Sir John Clifford stepped from the press of soldiers and thrust out his arm in front of Butler's man, stopping him from approaching the Duke. He stared down at the body of York, his teeth gritted, bloodshot eyes wild and starting from his head. "No...no, do not touch him...York is mine. Mine. I want vengeance for my slain kin. It is my right to take his head..."

Butler grimaced and turned away; Clifford's was not the normal behaviour of a knight; he needed to be stopped. But Clifford was strong-willed and swift. Muscling Butler's foot soldier aside, his sword slashed down and a deeper red stained the snow. Face contorted in a snarl, seeming scarcely human, he raised his gory trophy up by the hair. "Let the Duke of York go to York and gaze down from Micklegate Bar."

He then thrust the head towards the still-gaping soldier, who fumbled with it, horrified. "Take it, her Grace the Queen will want proof that her most foul enemy is dead. And I...I have one more thing to do this day. One more thing."

While the Yorkist dead were despoiled of armour and other items of value, young Edward of Rutland galloped madly towards the town of Wakefield. Many in Wakefield were loyal adherents of the Duke; surely, someone would shield him, York's son, by offering him refuge in some hidden cellar or attic room?

Tears stung his eyes, along with fleeting flakes of snow; he knew his father was dead, had seen him go down in a press of enemy bodies, overwhelmed. At the last, he had called to him, "Fly, fly, boy! Ride for your life!"

Loyally he had done his sire's bidding, one last time, disengaging from his first serious battle and taking horse alongside his tutor, the priest Robert Aspell. Down across the bloodstained snow the two fugitives raced, fleeing towards the town, their solitary hope of sanctuary...

Wakefield Bridge loomed, its graceful arches fording the winter-swollen, grey waters of the Calder. Against the sky, the finials of the bridge chapel of St Mary the Virgin thrust up like thin needles stitching the ever-lowering clouds. The hooves of Edmund's horse clattered on the icy cobblestones, striking sparks in the fury of his speed. Soon…just a little bit further…he would be there…

Suddenly, in the gloom ahead appeared a row of armoured men, a line of metallic death blocking the town end of the bridge—blocking the road to freedom, to safety. Bows and pikes were directed towards him. The Lancastrians must have sent extra men to the bridge to bar any flight into town after the rout. They wanted no survivors.

Edmund dragged on his steed's reins, pulling the animal to an abrupt stop, making it slide dangerously on the impacted snow. Leaping from its back, he began to run for the door of the chantry chapel, his only hope. It was not a designated sanctuary but his foes might respect the sanctity of a church and not commit violence there.

Might.

Behind him, all too close, he heard his tutor's shout of fear. "No, no, do not harm him, I beg you! He is but a boy and the son of a prince; his family will pay ransom…"

"I want no ransom; I want my revenge."

Edmund whirled around just as Sir John Clifford, smeared with the gore of the battlefield, sprang from his steed and strode swiftly, purposefully, towards him. He looked like a creature from hell, blood-encrusted, his visor up and his look crazed, pitiless, inhuman.

"As your father slew mine, so I shall slay you, boy!" he shouted, and in his gauntleted hand appeared a rondel dagger, shining like a wan star in the dim wintry light.

Edmund raised a hand to block his opponent's blow, but Clifford had years of experience in brutal warfare, whereas the second son of York, at seventeen, had none. Driven with all the force of Clifford's rage, the dagger pierced through the join of his armour beneath his left arm.

It was strange. At first, he felt no pain; it was hard to believe he had been stabbed. Then a wave of dizziness swept over him, and he found himself unable to speak. He crashed to his knees as Clifford caught him in a deadly grip and thrust the knife into his side again and again until, at the last, the blade itself snapped off in the wound. Then, with a satisfied grunt, Clifford flung the fatally wounded youth down upon the cobbles.

Coldness seeped through Edmund's body and he writhed on the ice and packed snow, hand stretching in a futile gesture towards the elusive door of the Chapel. The statures of saints, age-blackened, gazed down with sorrowful eyes rimmed by a haze of snow. Their faces seemed gaunt, skull-like, and reminiscent of death. Above them, the Blessed Virgin wept snowflake tears.

Edmund's own eyes were growing dim; loud ringing sounded in his ears. From a great distance, he could see his father, his father whom he knew was dead, standing in a shining circle of light, dressed in his fine armour but bare-headed...he held out a hand as if to guide him home. Even further away, held fast in webs of shadow, stood his mother and his numerous sisters and brothers; Edward, the closest to him in age and his good friend throughout their boyhood, towered about them all the rest, a giant of a youth with a face both fair and merry.

"Edward..." Wondering at how weak his voice was, he fought to wrench words from his constricting throat, "Avenge me, avenge father...be the King...*Be the King.*"

Then his reaching hand touched that of the light-wreathed vision of his dead father...and the utter darkness and eternal peace enfolded him.

Chapter 2

Edward of March was in the town of Gloucester, where he had celebrated Christmas with much feasting and revelry. He was also in bed with a beautiful but wanton girl he had snatched from the banquet and hustled into the inn where he was staying.

After romping for many an hour in the large, curtained bed, the young nobleman and his doxy both fell into a languorous, sated sleep…but suddenly something awoke Edward, making him sit bolt upright in the dark. The girl beside him mumbled inaudibly and dragged the counterpane closer to her ample curves.

Edward had felt a flash of coldness, a chill that reached for his very heart. It was as if dead men's spirits had run straight through him, flesh and bone. Spirits that called to him, *"Arise, arise!"*

Clambering uneasily to his feet, he flung a robe around his towering frame and went to the window of the tavern where he lodged. Outside the sky was paling from black to blue, heralding dawn; a thin stream of snowflakes spiralled down to land on the cobblestones below. Far away, through the morning's murk, the towers of St Peter's abbey gleamed against the sky, pale gold in a world of grey, white and blue.

Edward breathed a sigh of relief; the town yet slept, as did willing young Jocosa lying in the bed, her hair spread across the bolster like a river of gold. His premonition was merely an ill humour of the night, imaginary, unreal…He would return to the pleasant warmth of both bed and bawd, and muse no more on dark imaginings.

He had started to turn back to Jocosa when he heard it—a horse's hooves striking cobbles outside at high speed. Lunging for the window, he dragged the shutters open wide and leaned out into the dawn-light, the snow frosting his mane of hair and clinging to his lashes.

Into the street beyond the inn, a man on horseback came riding, as if blown in on the winter winds. He looked like the harbinger of doom from some ancient tale—his helmet dinted from blows, his cloak torn and slashed, fluttering like a tattered shroud. Immediately Edward's keen eyes picked out the badge upon the rider's shoulder. The Falcon and Fetterlock—the badge of his father, the Duke of York. He then took in the colour of the man's garb—Murrey and Blue, the colours of the House of York. Lastly, and with a sick feeling, he noted that the man's upturned face was battered and bloodied; and that old, dried blood marred his clothes in huge blackened patches. The horse beneath him was lathered, half-dead from exertion, its trembling legs coated with clots of mud.

The appropriate action would have been to send servants down to escort the stranger into the inn, but filled with sudden, unwarranted fear, Edward had no inclination for propriety.

"You there, down below!" he shouted, gesturing to the battered figure in Murrey and Blue. Behind him, woken by his shout, Jocosa uttered a sharp little shriek and stared fearfully over at Edward. She began to speak but he waved his hand irritably at her, gesturing for her to be silent.

The man in York colours reined in his mount and slid from the saddle, letting the reins trail on the cobbles. Gasping, head wreathed by the mist of his breath, he stood staring up at Edward. Staring dumbly, as if his someone had torn out his tongue.

"Speak! Speak!" Edward struck the windowpane with his hand. "Why do you not speak? I see that you wear my father's badge."

Painfully the man swallowed and bowed his head; his words tumbled forth, broken, halting. "My Lord, I bear ill-tidings from Sandal Castle. His Grace the Duke was deceived by the Queen's men with promises of a Christmas truce. He was lured out from the castle and most treacherously slain."

"Jesu!" cried Edward, the pain of loss ripping into him, sharp as a blade. "And my brother...my brother Edmund...Where is he?"

The man's head drooped even further; tears began to track through the heavy grime on his face. "My Lord, he was slain also, flying for Wakefield town by way of the bridge. They say it was John Clifford who did the deed; men are calling him 'the Butcher.'"

Edward felt his head spin in shock, nearly spilling him to the floor but then red rage overtook him. Fury burned hot as a brand, consuming heart and soul. "Edmund...he was but seventeen. *Seventeen!* God help me, I shall wreak vengeance on those who have committed this act! I swear, by Christ on the Cross, I will have my revenge. Unlike my poor, late father, I will not seek merely to be the eventual heir to that mad fool, Henry Six...I will take his crown *now*, and woe to him who stands in my path. With my sire's passing, I am Duke of York as well as Earl of March...but soon I will be King of all England!"

Edward rode steadily along the beautiful but treacherous Welsh Border, gathering forces to stave off the host of Jasper Tudor, Earl of

Pembroke. As he journeyed from one remote manor to the next, his handsome presence and genial, open manner soon brought men flocking to the White Rose of York. The Rose of Rouen they called him, for his birthplace and for his great masculine beauty—well over six feet tall, he towered over most men while his face was fair and his eyes sharp and clear. He was only eighteen years old, just one year older than Edmund who had died so horribly on the snow-and-blood slimed bridge at Wakefield.

Riding through the freezing fog of yet another bitter January morning, he thought of his brother, lost forever. They had been as close as brothers could be while growing up at Ludlow Castle; no strife ever brewed between them, even though their father favoured Edmund, whom he resembled much more closely in looks and mannerisms. Silly as young lads often were when together, they had terrorised their tutors, played schoolboy pranks to annoy the cook and servants, and wrote begging letters to the Duke for green gowns, prayerbooks and new bonnets. Their pleas to the Duke were not always for themselves, however—once they even asked their father to help the Croft brothers, Richard and Thomas, who were suffering odious maltreatment from certain members of the household staff.

Many a young man might have wept at such memories but Edward's jaw tensed with anger instead. Steel was in his heart; he had no time to weep. He must stop the Lancastrian army under Tudor from entering England and marching towards London as his spies had warned him was Jasper's intent. Margaret of Anjou was already hastening from the north, burning and looting towns in her wake—her host had gutted Beverley, among many other places. Edward was relying on Warwick to hold her from the capital and to keep the imprisoned King Henry, weak as a mewling lamb and spouting endless jumbled prayers, out of his fiercely determined wife's hands.

"I will have my vengeance," he murmured to himself, repeating it like one of Mad Harry's prayers. He thought of his mother, Duchess Cecily, and his sister and two younger brothers in London; safe, for the moment behind the stout walls of Baynard's castle. God only knew how they were dealing with the news of the Duke's death and the uncertainty of their position; he had advised his mother to send the boys abroad for their own safety and that of the House of York. For if he were to fail in his endeavour to claim the Crown, they must assume his role...

He shook his head, deep in memory. Why had his father made such rash choices, both in his claim to the throne and during his last battle at Wakefield? When the Duke had returned from brief exile in Ireland after fleeing the disaster at Ludford Bridge, he had taken counsel with neither Edward nor the Earl of Warwick, nor anyone else. Cold and aloof, telling none his plans, he had marched into the throne room at Westminster and placed his hand upon the empty throne in an act of possession that shocked everyone, including Edward. He, Edmund and Warwick had swiftly joined the other lords in convincing the Duke that his action was not the way. Richard had backed off, leaving the hall with a face like thunder, but then had broken into the King's apartments and sequestered himself inside. Later, a barely lucid King Henry had tremulously agreed to make the Duke and his sons heirs to the throne, effectively disinheriting his own young son, Edward of Lancaster.

That was what had raised the ire of Henry's devil-wife, Margaret, the French woman. Men said never to threaten the cub of a wolf, and so it was with Margaret of Anjou. She would not accept that her weak-willed husband cast away her son's birthright so easily, and her treacherous followers had brought death to Richard Duke of York...and Edmund of Rutland....

Rage tore through Edward's breast again and he struck his spurs into his mount's sides, driving it forward in a prancing of hooves. He was on the lands of his old friends, the Crofts, and through the grey murk of morning, he spied the dim outline of their castle keep in the distance, the banners on the turrets hanging limp after the night's bitter sleet.

They would help him. They remembered the Duke of York with kindness...and his sons who had stood up against the bullying of the Croft boys. They would gather stout men—pikemen, spearmen, halberdiers, archers with man-high bows of yew. The Crofts would help him take his bloody revenge...and assume the Mad King's crown.

Chapter 3

Sleet drove down on the stony bastions of Wigmore castle, one of the primary holdings of the Mortimer family, Edward of York's ancestors. A towering figure in his armour, Edward rode out from the great, ironbound gate next to the smaller figure of Sir Richard Croft on his bay destrier. Grim-faced, Croft's two sons, once in knightly training alongside Edward and Edmund at Ludlow, trotted a few paces behind their father. Will Hastings, Edward's close friend despite an age gap of over ten years, rode with them. Banners flying, a large host followed them—the lords of the Marches and their men.

"I am depending on you, Sir Richard," said Edward, glancing over at the knight. "You know this land well, far better than I do. I know it only for a treacherous land full of bogs that drag men down to eternity, and rivers that break their banks in winter and swallow all in their wake."

"I will do my best to assist you, your Grace," said old Richard Croft. "Neither weather nor terrain will hold us back. What does your intelligence say? From whence do you believe our enemies will come?"

Deep in thought, Edward frowned, recalling news his loyal scouts had brought to him. "Jasper Tudor will, I deem, head to the river Lugg and seek to cross with his forces. I aim to stop him and keep the bridge to my back."

"Who leads the Lancastrians besides Tudor of Pembroke?" Will Hastings leaned over his horse's snow and ice speckled mane and raised his voice above the shrill shriek of the wind. "What are we facing here, Ned?"

"Jasper Tudor is a skilled soldier and our greatest threat, I would wager." Edward stared out over the muted landscape that rolled into the distance. "My spies tell me his chief commanders include James Butler..."

"Butler? The Flying Earl?" yelped Will, an amiable man with a long face and nose, and eyes that were bright and quick—especially when they alighted on a beautiful woman, although at present there were no such ladies for Hastings to ogle. "You mean he who is noted for his frequent flights from the field? They say he fears the thick of battle in case it spoils his pretty looks. He leads his men in...but if things turn particularly nasty, he's away."

"Yes, that's him, the Earl of Ormonde...that craven dog." Edward's mouth thinned to a grim line. "And I have a special bone to pick with that particular dog—for he was commander on that black day at Wakefield when my father was slain." Reaching down to his side, he grasped the hilt of his sword meaningfully "He was there...at the last. He didn't flee *that* day, God curse him."

Releasing his swordhilt, he continued in a low voice. "There is also Owen, the greybeard, the old Tudor. Jasper's father."

"The one who tupped the old French Queen, old Harry Five's wife!" Hastings smirked as he remembered the scandal. "Lucky old Welsh goat!"

"Yes, that's him, and he was said to have married Catherine...but who knows?" Edward let out a bitter laugh. "It was all done in secret, after all."

"The sky is darkening," interrupted Sir Richard Croft, staring up at the heavens. "Let us be on our way, my Lord Edward, ere the weather worsens. If we do not make haste, our enemies will. We must meet them with fury and swiftness, and not allow them to pass into the south."

Edward's army proceeded, marching onwards in the dark, frosted morning when the entire world seemed dead and cold. Besides Will Hastings and the Croft family, long-time Yorkist stalwarts, he had the backing of such powerful nobles as John Tuchet Lord Audley, Reginald Grey Baron Wilton, Sir William Herbert of Raglan, Sir Walter Devereux Baron Ferrers and Humphrey Stafford of Grafton. Overall, their combined soldiers probably numbered more than their Lancastrian foes, but Jasper Tudor had a reputation as a fierce warrior and canny tactician. Edward was impressive to behold and full of the fury of his righteous cause...but he was still very young, and relatively untried. With the Earl of Warwick, he had proven victorious at Northampton but it was the defection of Lord Grey to the Yorkist cause that had brought about their swift, brutal victory, in which Humphrey Stafford, Duke of Buckingham and other great lords had fallen defending Mad Harry's tent while the King quivered inside.

The way across the border country was stony, the wind howling across those desolate, debatable lands. Trees stood ragged in the gloom, their branches swinging like the flailing arms of fleshless skeletons. Strewn rose like twisted heads, bones of giants trapped in the earth. It was a nightmare world of coldness, a haunted landscape soaked in primal myth and legend.

Gradually, however, the horizon began to lighten and the oppressive cloud-cover tore asunder, revealing a faded, icy-blue dawn sky. In the east, the sun began a swift ascent, its pallid golden light striking the winter-bound land...but then, abruptly, it changed. Murmurs ran throughout Edward's forces; the foot soldiers and archers stopped dead in their tracks, pointing at the sky. Full of consternation, Edward peered heavenward, shielding his eyes with a hand.

Above him in the firmament, he witnessed the strangest sight he had ever seen in his young life. The sun had risen in all its usual fiery splendour but on either side of it glowed two smaller, red-rimmed suns under an all-encompassing halo.

Three Suns shone in the sky near the village of Mortimer's Cross upon that Candlemas morning...

At Edward's back there were noises of fearful men and agitated horses. Soldiers crossed themselves, looking uneasy. "Tisn't natural!" Edward heard one say, his voice carried to his lord's ears on the stiff breeze. "God is sending us a sign that the day will be lost. These three suns are an evil omen! An omen of death!"

A surge of panic shot through the young commander. He knew he the strangeness of the morning sky might make the common soldiers lose heart. At worst, they might desert, at best they would fight half-heartedly, believing themselves already doomed. Neither prospect was appealing. Without courage and fervent support, he would lose the day; perhaps lose everything, even his life...

"Hold my banner on high!" he ordered his standard-bearer, and as the man obeyed, the Lion of March flared out across the sky, the lion's claws seeming to stretch toward those ominous suns above. Edward drove his steed forward and rose in the stirrups so that all men could clearly see their leader. Drawing his sword, the light of the Three Suns caught on the edge of the great blade and turned it to lambent flame.

Lifting his visor, he spoke, his words ringing out into the cold morn, "Good, true men of England, be not afraid of what you see! The strange symbols in the sky are surely sent from God Almighty as a token of our victory. Look at them and behold, there are three suns—is that not representative of the Holy Trinity, the Father, the Son and the Holy Ghost? This sign also betokens the ascendancy of Three Sons of

York, who live on after their noble father, the true sons of Royal blood!"

The men's muttering changed, began to sound more positive. The Holy Trinity—yes, yes, it *could* be a sign from God, a positive sign rather than a token of defeat and death. And there *were* three sons of York for their leader had two younger brothers, George and Richard.

Edward could sense confidence returning to the host, the desire to take on the enemy and win. He brandished his blade once again, looking every inch the warrior-hero. "Forward, forward, in the name of the Blessed Virgin and St George! I commend my cause to God, and if I win this day, forever my token shall be the Sun in Splendour as it was seen above Mortimer's Cross..."

A ragged shout came from the men in the Yorkist army, and now they gazed at the miracle in the heavens with new, awe-filled eyes. Some raised the hilts of their swords to their lips and reverently kissed the cross. Above, the eerie Three Suns kept burning, pale flames in the burgeoning light.

It was time to engage the enemy.

Edward's force moved forward slowly, decisively. The archers broke away, heading out to rising ground where they could pick off any approaching soldiers.

Ahead the dawn mists were parting, tearing apart like winding sheets, as figures emerged from this greyness, some mounted, most on foot. The banners of Pembroke and his allies fluttered in the chill February wind, Tudor's bearing the lilies of France and the lions of England, surrounded by a blue border filled with golden martlets.

Edward seethed at the sight of these near-Royal Arms, granted by Mad Harry to his half-brothers. This was the hour of the day...the day Edward of March, now Duke of York and heir to England, would begin his quest for revenge. His quest for a crown.

"Advance banners!" he cried sternly, raising a gauntleted hand, and his men marched with intent towards the Lancastrian front line.

As in most battles of the time, there were three divisions amongst the opposing armies—the left 'battle', the right and the centre. The Flying Earl, James Butler, was the first to launch his battle at the forces of the young Duke of York. The fighting quickly became fierce, men striving against each other and hacking at their foes with fury. Edward's well-placed archers sought to pick off enemy soldiers before they joined the melee, but despite their best efforts, Butler's men forced the right wing of Edward's army back in the direction they had come. The

Lancastrians let out a roaring cheer and thrust forward, eager to break the line and start a rout.

Under Lord Devereux, the Yorkists fought desperately to hold their ground, not giving up one more inch of ground to their adversaries. Unable to keep its impetus, Butler's own wing began to dissipate, the men becoming separated and then surrounded, or else picked off by the keen-eyed Yorkist archers.

The Earl of Wiltshire stared in alarm as his wing collapsed. Many of his soldiers were poorly armed Irish levies, and seeing the way the wind was blowing, they wavered and then scattered, fanning out across the bleak landscape where the Yorkist archers swiftly brought them down.

James Butler put up his sword and began to run, thrusting foot soldiers aside and shouting to his squires for assistance. A fresh horse was dragged through the milling press of bodies, and true to his reputation, the flying Earl flung himself into the saddle and galloped away from the field, leaving his men to face destruction.

Edward was barely aware of this development, however. Taking the centre division, he had engaged with Pembroke, who, being the most experienced tactician of the Lancastrian lords, commanded the Lancastrian centre. With great blows, the young giant launched himself at the front line of Pembroke's division, and men fell screaming before his wrath, unable to withstand the violence of his mighty blows. Terrifying, armed with sword and mace, he charged into his opponents, smashing the heads of the shortest ones as if they were over-ripe fruits. Steadily he held his ground, perched on a defensive wall of broken corpses as the battle surged around him and the earth beneath his adversaries' feet became a churned sea of mud and blood.

For some time, neither of the two centres could gain any clear advantage, despite Edward's valour and strength of arms. Then Owen Tudor, the ageing father of Jasper, attempted to bring his wing around and circle the Yorkist left, hoping to strike a deadly blow to the flank. The old warrior's move failed utterly. The air darkened with Yorkist arrows, picking off the foremost of his men. Hand gonnes and several cannons roared, filling the cold air with rancid smoke and adding to the terror and confusion on the field.

Owen's wing began to dissolve, his men turning and running along the nearby riverbank, where Edward's archers took more of them down. Bodies splashed into the river, crashing through the thin rim of ice and bobbing gruesomely along on the swell. The breaking of

Owen's embattled wing quickly turned into a full-blown rout, with the Yorkists pursuing the Lancastrians and hewing them down as they fled.

Now Jasper Tudor's centre began to dissolve, crumbling beneath Edward's incessant onslaught of sword, bill, halberd and pike. More Lancastrians started to flee the battlefield. Tudor, realising the day was almost certainly lost, managed to extricate himself from the heaving bodies and find his steed. He galloped from the field, leaving the Yorkists to slaughter any man not swift enough or lucky enough to get away.

By dusk on St Blaise's day, the fighting was done. Dead men lay sprawled on the icy ground, heaps of red, hewn flesh, as they were divested or their armour and any goods they might own—rings, good luck relics, pendants, ampullae filled with holy water from sacred shrines.

Satisfied, Edward stood amidst the carnage. It was a pity Pembroke and Wiltshire had managed to escape his wrath, but at the very least he had sent a strong message to his adversaries. The Duke of York's son was a force to be reckoned with. He would give no quarter to his foes.

Lifting off his great war helm, he let the cold air caress his sweat and blood-streaked face. It felt good upon his skin, as he took deep breaths, ignoring the stench of blood and the acrid aroma of the gonnes.

"My Lord Edward!" Glancing around, he saw William Herbert, known as Black William for his dark features, striding across the battlefield towards him. Herbert had been a great supporter of the Duke of York and had transferred his loyalty to his son.

"Herbert?" Edward raised an eyebrow. The man before him was full of ill-contained excitement.

"We've had news, my lord. A messenger has ridden in from Hereford. When Owen Tudor's men were routed, ours chased them all the way to the city. Most have been slain in the streets but some of them have been taken prisoner…including Owen Tudor."

Edward's lips drew back in a mirthless smile. "What justice. I have lost a father. So too shall Jasper Tudor."

Herbert glanced down, unable to meet the young man's hot gaze. He had supported Duke Richard…but was it not this seeking of personal revenge that had turned these tussles for supremacy between cousins into battles filled with bloody vengeance, where thousands died and chivalry died with them?

Edward noted Black William's sour expression. His eyes narrowed, gold and green fire in his wind-burnt face. "Owen Tudor is an old man, that is true," he said softly, "and some might find pity for him because of his age. But my brother Edmund...my dear, beloved companion of my youth...was only seventeen. No one took pity on him at Wakefield; none sought to still Butcher Clifford's hand. Remember that, Herbert. Remember."

"I will, my lord," said William Herbert, his voice as bleak as the landscape around them with its dead trees and dead men. So much death...He dearly wanted to say, *Be not hasty, my lord Edward, for you are only eighteen, not so much older*, but he dared not.

Edward slammed down his visor. "Let us ride for Hereford," came his muffled voice, made strangely inhuman by the metal encasing his head. "I now have urgent business there."

Chapter 4

Owen Tudor crouched in the dark of his cell in Hereford castle, listening to the rats and mice skittering through the hay spread on the freezing floor. He had not thought he would end up in a dungeon—a death on the field, perhaps, but not this ignominy, lying in filthy straw and ordure like a common criminal. He laughed bitterly—at least his son Jasper had escaped unharmed.

Sighing, he thought back on his eventful life—the day he had danced too strenuously, showing off his strong legs and agile moves... and had fallen into the inviting lap of Catherine, the Dowager Queen, relict of King Hal, victor of Agincourt, and mother of the boy-King Henry VI. How graceful Catherine had been, with her long swan's neck as white as snow, and her high, pale brow gleaming as if a star was bound upon it. She had laughed when he suspected admonishment, and a sparkle in her sea-blue eyes made him grow hot with unexpected desire. A passionate woman surely—men whispered she had lain with Edmund Beaufort, Duke of Somerset after the King's sad demise and so Humphrey of Gloucester enacted a law so that she could not marry without the King's consent...and the King was, at the time, but six.

He'd never asked her the truth about Edmund, not even after she had invited him to her apartments alone and said, in her husky French voice, "Will you dance for me again, Owen Tudor?" and they had ended up in a delicious tangle of discarded velvet and brocade. He was a little perplexed when Catherine, not so very long after their union, produced a fine healthy son...and, without any consultation with Owen, named him Edmund.

Young Edmund took the name of Tudor, no matter who his true father was, as did the other children that followed in due time, Jasper, Edward and Margaret—and it was only proper, for in secret Owen had married the Dowager Queen, just the two of them in a tiny chapel, with a nervous old priest and a solitary witness.

Owen had paid a high price for that illicit marriage to a woman far above his station. When Catherine died after a hard childbirth in which the infant also died, Owen was charged with the offence of marrying the Dowager Queen without consent and hauled away to Newgate prison. His children were taken to be raised by the Abbess of Barking, Katherine de la Pole.

And now here he was in prison again, this time in the stinking cells of Hereford Castle. But he would come through it. He had survived before. He'd been bailed from Newgate and had a complete reversal of his misfortunes, becoming an important member of Henry VI's household. Henry admired and grew to love his two half-brothers, Edmund and Jasper, and saw that they received titles as a token of his affection. (Edward had become a monk and died young, God assoil him; Margaret was a nun.)

Despite being on opposing sides, he was quite sure Edward of March would show him clemency. He could be ransomed off. York probably needed the money and Jasper was a generous boy—he would pay handsomely for his father's safety and freedom. However, a cold fear began to gnaw at his innards, made worse by the frigid drafts winding through chinks in the stone walls of his cell. What…what if Edward sought revenge? He…he wanted to live…in his old age, he'd found another mistress, bringing unexpected comfort in the lonely years after Catherine's death. To his joy, she had not long before produced his last-born son, the child of his old age. Little David was only two years old…

A noise in the corridor beyond the stout cell door broke Owen's troubled thoughts. Footsteps sounded on the flagstones beyond, hurried and purposeful. They were coming for him, maybe to take him to March, maybe…Sweat began to bead on the back of his neck, beneath his lank greying hair.

No, no, they would not harm him! King Henry was his elder boys' half-brother, and Henry still ruled, no matter the pretensions of the eldest boy of the dead Duke of York's …

But Edward of March, heir of York, had won the battle at Mortimer's cross…He was a boy no longer…and what else could he win in time?

A key ground in a lock and a bolt shot back with an unnerving bang. Armoured men filed into the cell, the bright torchlight behind their heads making Owen shield his eyes with his hand.

"Up with you!" A soldier jabbed at him with the butt of a pike. "His Grace the Lord Edward wants to see you."

"What for? He cannot try me, he's no King! —I fought for my rightful King!" Owen mustered up all the defiance he could.

"The crown is on the head of the wrong man," smirked the soldier, "but not for long I'll warrant. So hold your tongue, Welshman."

Owen was led through the bowels of Hereford Castle to the Great Hall. The smells of food first made him hungry, and then retch as the seriousness of his dire situation hit home. All around were hostile faces, mocking faces, and at the head of the room, on a raised dais, lounged the would-be usurper, York's son, regarding him with cold eyes.

How handsome was the young man on the high seat, his hair haloed by the torchlight and his chain of office gleaming on a chest as broad as an oak. And so young...so *young*...and yet somehow so terrifying. He was dressed gaudily, a red robe trimmed with marten fur, long-toed shoes capped with silver, a doublet of sky blue stitched with York roses and the Fetterlock of his father but no popinjay was Edward of March. His face was intelligent, his demeanour sombre...and deadly. There was a cold ruthlessness in his expression, belying his youth and masculine beauty.

"Owen Tudor..." He leaned back and sipped from a goblet. "So today I meet the wily Welshman who bedded a Queen. Little good has her embraces brought you, I fear. Today you will rue the day you fell under her spell and spawned Pembroke who fought against meat Mortimer's Cross. What words have you to say to that?"

There were no words the Welshman could say. None.

Edward sighed, looking suddenly bored with the whole proceedings. He made a small gesture with his hand to the soldiers that stood, hovering ominously, at Owen's back.

The old man found himself being rushed out of the castle and along the cobbled high street of Hereford. On either side, the people of the town roared and shrieked, their voices rising in wails like the ululations of a host of demons. Edward of March's men thrust at them with pikes and bills, keeping them as far away from Owen as possible. It gave the captured man some small comfort to see that they were displeased by his harsh treatment.

Two soldiers were holding Owen; tall warriors clad from head to toe in armour. Their visors were down; he could not see their faces. Grasping him by either arm, they dragged him along like a heavy sack, letting his dangling feet just skim the ground. Looking down, he noted there was blood curdled on the cobbles, filling the air with the sickly iron tang of the butcher's shop.

Up ahead, he could see a scaffold, newly erected, but its boards already awash with gore. The other captives from Mortimer's Cross had already been executed, it seemed. He was the last, the only one alive.

Nervously he glanced around. Would March be there? Surely, the message would come that he would be spared. He was old, and although he served in the King's household he was not personally involved in any feud. This was just a warning, an effort to frighten him, a message to his son Jasper about what might happen...

Dizzy and flailing, he was pushed up the steps of the scaffold and forced onto his knees before a crude block of wood soaked with the gore of the last man who died upon it.

Shuddering, he knelt, blinking up at the sun high above in the morning sky. "Have...have you not done enough?" he croaked to any who could hear. "Let me up. I have surrendered. The King and my son Jasper will ransom me. I will speak to them of Edward of York's might and how terms mush swiftly be reached. I..."

"Be silent, old man." The headsman appeared, a vast shadow that blocked out the sunlight. "You will never get up again." Reaching down, he grasped the collar of Owen's red doublet and roughly ripped it away.

Owen gasped, stunned by the sudden realisation of what was happening. There would be no reprieve, no pardon. He would feel the bite of the axe as surely as any of the other prisoners.

The old ways were done. Vengeance ruled supreme.

Cruel hands pushed him forward till he lay fully over the saturated block. Closing his eyes, he sent his last prayers heavenward. Dully, with quaking tongue, he murmured his final words, "Ah...to think that the head that once lay on Queen Catherine's lap has ended up adorning this filthy block!"

The axe flashed down. The crowd in Hereford market square shrieked and roared, some in pity and dismay, others with a newfound lust for blood. No matter which side lost, a good beheading was always seen as a cause for excitement.

Edward stood in Hereford marketplace with William Hastings and a party of his stalwarts. Twilight had fallen, casting an eerie violet glow over the timber-framed buildings that leaned over the square. The cobbles gleamed wetly where they had been sluiced with water to remove the blood from the executions.

In the centre of the square, near the towering market cross, knelt a distraught woman, her hair a wild tangle of yellow streaked with crimson, her dress rumpled and stained with gore. She sat within a ring of tapers, their flames flickering wanly in the gloom like those of tricksy corpse-candles in a marsh, and in her hands she held the gaping, bloodied head of Owen Tudor.

Back and forth she rocked, crooning, wiping at the livid face and combing the clotted hair with her fingers. "Poor Owen Tudor," she crooned. "If your Catherine could not be here to hold ye, I will."

"A mad woman." Hastings crossed himself. "Lighting the candles in such a manner just after Candlemas—could it be considered an act of sacrilege?"

"Whatever it is, leave her be; she harms none," said Edward. "But how did she get a hold of the traitor's head in the first instance?"

"Some say she was his mistress, the mother of his lastborn bastard. It was given her out of pity."

Edward glanced towards the keening woman with a vague trace of sympathy. Unlike some of his royal forebears in ages past, he did not make war on women. Except for Queen Margaret, of course, a woman whose fierceness made her an unnatural creature. But not those who were powerless. "Let the wench, whoever she be, have him to do with what she will and to arrange for his burial. The Greyfriars will doubtless take the body in."

The young Duke turned from the strange, unsavoury sight on the market cross and beckoned to his followers for a horse. "We must not tarry here any longer. We shall head towards Gloucester and await news from my cousin Warwick in the south."

Hastings blinked. "Should we not march to his aid, having had this great victory? Although the men are weary…"

Edward shook his head. "As you said, the men are weary. There is no need at present to push them beyond endurance. Warwick will manage well enough on his own—he is a great captain, while I am still new to this business of war. I will await his instructions, Will. I am certain prudence in this matter is for the best."

Edward's party left the market square, seeking the road to Gloucester. Behind him, the woman on the cross continued to keen as the moon, rising above the shoulders of the houses, shone cold blue on the surface on Owen Tudor's dead eyes.

Richard Neville, Earl of Warwick, marched his army towards St Albans. He was late and he knew it. He did not know what had possessed him to delay in London so long. There was business to attend to, certainly—he had made his brother John Lord Montagu and assumed his father's former position as Great Chamberlain. And then there had been the Garter ceremony, called in the palace of the Bishop of London—with all the pomp he could muster, he was elected to the Order along with the lords Wenlock, Bonville and Kyriell. Necessary, to show themselves to the people as great lords of the realm…but he was late. Margaret of Anjou's army was nearing London, and towns and villages burned in her wake—Stamford was gutted, Grantham burnt.

The Earl's army neared the ancient town that was his destination, a Roman town where ancient mosaics still turned up beneath the plough in the very shadow of the great Abbey with its shrines to St Alban and St Amphibalus. Warwick remembered St Alban's well; he had fought there once before, creeping over fences and through yards until he was able to attack the unsuspecting Lancastrian hovering in the market square. That day had gone well, with Edmund Beaufort and the Earl of Northumberland and Baron Clifford all slain and the King and Buckingham wounded.

He prayed his luck would hold again.

Warwick's line of men began the hilly ascent into the town. On either side of the road the terrified townsfolk scrambled into their houses, barricading themselves behind their doors, although they knew that if either of the combatants decided to fire the town, their fate would be the flames.

Warwick ignored the scattered of fearful townsfolk, leading his troops in a blare of trumpets past the stern bulk of the Abbey to the far edge of the town. His captains—Norfolk, Arundel, Montagu, Bonville—followed with banners raised.

There Warwick spread his forces out as far as No Man's Land near the village of Sandridge. He hoped they would form a net of steel in which the hordes of Queen Margaret would be caught. His soldiers would block all the roads coming down from Luton.

The Earl grinned to himself as his soldiers dispersed to their allotted positions. He was a modern man and a modern warrior. Be damned the old ideals of chivalry—it was a new age now, a more brutal age. Going with this idea, he had brought all the newest devices of warfare to help in his endeavour—pavisses, wooden barricades and nets full of nails; and hand gonnes from Burgundy, some firing leaden balls, other blasting out wild fire. Best of all and most ingenious, he deemed, were the caltrops, iron balls with spikes that were planted along all routes into town. Man and beast alike would go down if they inadvertently stepped upon a caltrop.

Warwick's smugness over his weaponry stores vanished as a scout rode in, horse shuddering under him and visage white with fear. "My lord of Warwick, the Queen's army has overrun Dunstable and is marching hither at great speed following Watling Street. They will be here all too soon."

Warwick's face took on a grim cast. "Let them come, then. I will send the archers to halt their progress."

At that moment, there was a yelp from a striped pavilion set up beneath a nearby oak tree. Peevishly, Warwick glanced towards it. Inside was Henry VI, King of England. Warwick had brought the old madman for safety's sake, just in case someone in London turned their coast and tried to rescue him or use him to rally Lancastrian sympathisers. But he feared he would be a nuisance, and Harry Six was exactly that, blubbering and singing to himself between litanies of chanted prayers.

An old, long, sheep-like face with dim, unfocussed eyes poked out of the flaps of the tent. It was the King himself, greasy and unshaven, food smeared down the front of his robe. "Lord Warwick, Lord Warwick!" he cried, his voice high-pitched, a bird's twitter.

"Your Grace, what do you require?" asked Warwick between gritted teeth. He had greater things to attend to than placating this dotard!

"My wife! Where is my wife? Is Margaret here? Where is my wife?"

Warwick wiped a hand across his brow in frustration. He did not need histrionics from the King now. He forced a civil tone into his voice. "She…is otherwise engaged, your Grace. She comes, however…" *but God willing, you will never see her again…*

The King's face fell; he wrung his hands. "Oh, I do wish she would make haste…she sees things so much clearer than I do…This will not do, will not. And I am hungry, so very hungry…"

Warwick used the old man's wandering mind as a distraction. "Hungry, your Grace? If you would step back into your pavilion and becalm yourself, I will have the most tempting delicacies sent to you."

A wobbly smile crossed the King's crusted lips. "So be it. Very good. I am so so hungry, I tell you…"

The tent flap fell shut and Warwick sighed in relief. He beckoned Lord Bonville and Lord Kyriell over. "Don't let him out again," he ordered. "Stay here, I bid you, and guard the tent well. Margaret of Anjou draws nigh, and I don't want Henry drawing unwanted attention."

The Queen's advance guard reached St Alban's before dawn the next day, breaking into the northwestern side of the town. Warwick had already deployed his archers to meet them; arrows flew so thickly they blotted out the rising sun in a black, obscuring hail. But the archers could not hold the advantage for long—the Lancastrian army continued their attack from fields to the north of the town and managed to push on up into St Peter's street, one of St Albans' main thoroughfares. Shouting and whooping in bloodlust, they descended upon Warwick's archers and dispatched them without mercy.

Warwick ground his teeth in rage as he saw his archers decimated, the remainder fleeing through the barricaded town. Scouts had reported that Margaret's forces were a good three thousand greater than his own. He could scarcely afford to lose his trusted archers.

"Turn around, turn around! He shouted, rising in his stirrups, and gesturing to his foot soldiers and cavalry. "They attack is coming from a direction I did not anticipate. Swing round!"

Milling in confusion at this unexpected change, the army slowly turned. Montagu's wing had left its chosen vantage point and attempted to form a line facing the west, while Warwick tried to strengthen the line with soldiers from his centre.

In the midst of the confusion the Lancastrian host, sensing the uncertainty of the opposition, mounted a full attack on Montagu. Spotting the danger, Warwick rammed his own forces forward, offering reinforcement to his beleaguered brother. Montagu's line held though the fighting was fierce.

And then…*disaster.*

A Kentish captain called Henry Lovelace suddenly began marching away from the main body of the army with his men following in close formation. "You!" Warwick bellowed, his voice the roar of the angry bear emblazoned on his banners. "Halt!"

Lovelace glanced over his shoulder and raised his visor a crack. "I've given details of your battle plans to the Queen," he sneered. "The house of Lancaster pays me more than you do, Richard Neville…"

Enraged, Warwick swore a terrible oath and made to ride at the turncoat Lovelace, but one of his captains dragged him back.

The Lancastrian front uttered blood-curdling yells of triumph and poured forth into the hole formed in the Yorkist line with Lovelace's defection. Montagu could no longer hold his ground and his division began to dissolve into flight. All over the field, Margaret of Anjou's army was making inroads, separating the Yorkist factions and wreaking terrible carnage.

Warwick saw his brother's banner go down and Montagu vanish in a writhing sea of men, captured or worse. His heart sank. He could not regroup his forces; flight was now the only option.

He had lost.

Staring upwards, he noticed the dimness of the sky. Days were still short; darkness was falling, swift and complete. Thank God in heaven for that, at least! Maybe he could manage to slip away when enemy eyes were blinded by darkness. Hastily, he began giving the signals to retreat.

His host moved off into the growing gloom, the luckiest tramping to safety in the little lanes and forests areas around St Albans, the unlucky being chased by Lancastrian outriders up into the town where escape was remote. For a while, Warwick lingered on a rise overlooking the battlefield; he could see the King's tent, now surrounded by Lancastrians lords. The King was outside, waving his arms and capering about in his grubby robes like some mountebank. Warwick wondered what had become of the guards he'd set—the loyal Kyriell and Bonville. He could guess. If they were not already dead, they soon would be.

Setting spurs to his horse's flanks, he began an unhappy night journey toward the Midlands. He had to meet up with Edward…Edward, whom he had failed. How could he tell him?

Scowling and dispirited, the Earl led the remnants of his beaten army away into the freezing night, the cold rains of late winter lashing over them to add to their misery.

"My lord Edward…I am here, to throw myself on your mercy and accept your displeasure, as it must be." Richard Neville knelt before Edward of York in the small hall of a wayside inn at Chipping Norton and offered his sword hilt-first to the tall young man who stood before him.

Edward stared down at him impassively for a moment, then: "Get up, Dick. You have no need to do this."

"I failed you."

"Battles may be lost or won; such is the dictate of Fate. Mortimer's Cross was a great victory."

"It was indeed, thanks be to God…and to your own prowess. But Ned…" Warwick became informal now that he realised Edward bore him no ill will despite the catastrophe at St Albans. Edward was young but he knew well his cousin's worth. "The bitch-Queen's army will have reached London even as we speak. Curse that traitor Lovelace for going over to join her men! It…it is that evil rogue's fault this disaster has occurred."

"There's no need to speak of blame," said Edward, shortly. "We must devise our next move."

"Yes, yes, indeed we must," agreed Warwick, eager to turn the attention away from his shameful defeat.

"So…" Edward drew a dagger, began cleaning his nails with it. "Where is the King now?"

Warwick's mind leapt forward, quick as light. "King… The King is here before me. You are the King, Edward. You and no other."

Edward put down his dagger, stared into the fire burning in the ornate fireplace. Then he took a deep breath. "King Henry broke the Act of Accord when he left with Margaret. In all his actions, he shows himself no true King. His crown, therefore, is forfeit."

"Yes, yes, it is so!" Warwick clapped him on the shoulder in an over-familiar way, considering he had just declared the young man his King. "We must proceed on, and unseat him and his she-wolf of a Queen."

"Margaret of Anjou." Edward's voice was flat. "You were in London of late. What was the mood there ere you left? What do you think her reception will be? Will the Londoners cheer her and Mad Harry?"

Warwick hung his head, scowling. "Many in London were afraid; they heard the tales of how her army pillaged like Scots. Many support the House of York and lean towards you, but Margaret's army is powerful and she is fierce and cruel. When common men are faced with fear, who knows what they might do to save their own skins?"

At that moment, footsteps thundered on the outside steps leading to Edward's quarters. Both men looked questioningly towards the door and reached for their weapons.

"Will?" said Ned softly, making a motion towards the stout oak door with his head.

William Hastings, seated quietly by the fire whilst his friend spoke to Warwick, rose and approached the door, drawing his sword from its sheath at the same time. Pulling back the bolt with a clatter, he gazed into the hall beyond. "Who goes? Why do you disturb the Lord Edward?" he asked gruffly.

A muffled voice answered; Hastings slid out into the hall, then returned moments later, face flushed with relief. "Ned, there's news, *good* news..." He cast Warwick a meaningful look. "...from London."

A messenger stumbled into the chamber after Will, stiff-legged and mud-covered after the long ride. "Your Grace." He sank down before Edward's chair. "I bear great tidings of import. London has barred its gates against the Queen."

Edward's eyes widened. "Barred the gates?"

"Yes, my lord. The Londoners have no love of Margaret. When they heard of the defeat at St Albans, the merchants buried their wealth and shut up their houses. They were about to send out a surrender, though, for fear of what the Queen might do if they resisted, but then they learned that Margaret had remained in St Albans and sent much of her army back to Dunstable. There was no fear of being plundered anymore. High-handed as ever, Margaret demanded the city fathers send her food and gold, but before the carts could leave the city gates, the locals fell upon them, stealing both meat and money!"

Astounded, Edward stared, and then he began to laugh, great rolling peels of laughter. Hastings joined in and then even Warwick started to chuckle. "Would I could have seen the bitch's face when it was reported the supplies were stolen!" said Edward, wiping tears of mirth from the corners of his eyes. "For all that St Albans was a disaster, Fortune's Wheel turns again. There is hope."

Suddenly he grew serious, leaning forward in his seat with his smile waning. "Messenger, my mother, Duchess Cecily, is in London at Baynard's Castle. Is there any news from her?"

The messenger nodded. "Yes, my lord. Here…I have a missive for you from her Grace the Duchess." Reaching into the satchel fastened at his waist, he removed a rumpled parchment, hastily sealed and tied.

Edward took it, broke the seal, quickly read the contents and then folded up the letter. "My Lady Mother is in good spirits, as much as can be expected since it is not long since my sire's untimely death. She prays to God that soon full vengeance will be taken. She was fearful when she heard Margaret might enter London, but refused to leave the city before the approach of the termagant—however, acting upon my advice, she has sent my brothers George and Richard abroad to Burgundy for sake-keeping."

The young nobleman reached for his cloak, fastening it around his broad shoulders. "My Lady Mother's move was wise, but I deem my small brothers will be back in England before long. Get on your riding attire and summon your men, Warwick—must hurry to London at once. We must arrive while feeling against Queen Margaret is still high. The city folk cannot be permitted to change their minds in her favour."

"Let us go at once!" Warwick tightened his sword belt, yelled for squires to make ready the horses. In London, where he was well known and liked, he could surely prove his worth again. "We have no time to waste. And…" His lips drew back in a thin smile. "God save the King. King Edward, fourth of that name."

London simmered. The Queen had not moved towards them after she did not receive her asked-for supplies, yet she had not departed St Albans either. A Lancastrian delegation wearing the King's colours arrived with a warrant from old Harry; stern-faced and imperious, the well-guarded riders made their way towards the Guildhall, seeking the Mayor.

Local men pressed forward, nervous at seeing these lordly strangers with their faces hard as granite riding through the street with an air of authority. They circled them, crushing inwards and impeding their progress. The Lancastrians' frightened horses pranced and threw their heads; the guardsmen lowered their glinting pikes in a threatening manner, poking at the rabble.

"What is your business here in London?" a man shouted from a tavern door. Drawn by the commotion, angry Londoners with daggers and cudgels began to line the street; they blocked the Lancastrians' progress, uncaring that their opponents were much better armed.

"We have come to bring a warrant from his Grace, Henry VI, declaring Edward of March a traitor," sneered a knight who rode foremost amongst Queen Margaret's delegation. "Give way or we shall force you aside."

"Who do you think you are, telling us what to do, foreigner?" bellowed a man at the forefront of the hostile London crowd, and a quarterstaff sailed in the direction of one of the horse's skulls. "This ain't your city! Get back to your beloved she-wolf, the lot of you!"

A riot ensued. Fruit, dung and stones flew at the Lancastrian party. Enraged, they drew weapons and rode straight into the charging mob. A Londoner screamed and went down into the filthy gutter clutching a slashed face. Another was ridden down, his thighbone snapping with a nauseating sound as he fell onto the cobbles, writhing in agony.

The violence escalated; fighting turned into looting as the less savoury denizens of the city turned the fracas to their advantage. Londoners went rampaging through a nearby tavern, stealing kegs and assaulting the tavern wenches, while a nearby draper's shop was ransacked, the looters running out wrapped in rich cloths that flapped around them like sails.

Alarum bells started to ring in bell towers and people began yelling for the city bailiffs to bring order. Alerted to the disturbance, the Mayor of London came riding in surrounded by an armed guard that cast back the most aggressive rioters.

"I am putting a curfew on all London!" the Mayor bawled over the din of brawling men. "That is clearly the only way the King and his host can enter peacefully."

"We don't want the mad old git to enter!" raged a youth with a bloodied nose and a knife clenched in his fist. "We've had enough of him and that French harridan he wed! He's a loon and she's a whore who cuckolded 'im with Somerset!"

The Lancastrian delegation reacted with anger at this disparagement of King Henry and Queen Margaret. The Mayor, a large, rotund man not over-swift in his movements, was roughly thrust aside and the rioting and fighting resumed. Onlookers were beaten, doors kicked in and more shops raided. Rioters tried to climb onto the backs of the Lancastrian party's horses and bring their riders down.

"Guards!" the Mayor roared over the din, his face red with rage. "Forward! Stop this madness! Stop them!"

Immediately the heavily armoured city guards took an offensive position and without more ado crashed into rioters of both factions, using pikes and bills to drive the two sides apart.

At last, after a brief and bloody fray, a semblance of order resumed. The fractious Londoners were driven into the side streets and held there at sword point. Only the Lancastrian party remained in the main thoroughfare, bloody, battered, dishevelled—and angry.

Puffing and crimson-faced, the equally hostile Mayor faced them. "It is best if you go back whence you came. You are not welcome. I want peace in my city and you have brought bloodshed."

"What of the warrant given by the King?" The leader ripped a scroll from his saddlebag and waved it in the mayor's face as threateningly as any weapon. "The warrant that condemns March! It must be delivered!"

"Give it to me then, goddamn you!" Frustrated and fearful of renewed violence, the Mayor snatched the document from the man's hand, then looked at it as if he had grasped a scrap of offal. "It's not official, is it? Not under law. God's teeth, I thought not. London does not have to obey this warrant, you know…."

"You obstruct the King's wishes?" The leader of the Lancastrians bridled with wrath.

"I obey the law—you would do well to do the same. I obstruct no one. This warrant will be published only as a proclamation …and let the people of London make of it what they will. Now back off behind the city gates or I will have you all arrested as rioters and thieves!"

The Lancastrian party retreated, leaving London's Mayor with the unofficial warrant declaring Edward a traitor clutched in his hand.

As he began to retreat in the direction of Guildhall, one of the city Aldermen approached him. "Your Worship!" cried the man. "We must speak!"

"What is it? I must attend to this goddamned proclamation!" The Mayor brandished the scroll clutched in his fist.

"Outriders have brought news that Duke Edward is approaching London along with the Earl of Warwick and a mighty force."

The Mayor blanched, clutching the scroll to his chest. "Jesu! Will this madness never end?"

"They are asking for admittance to the city. What message shall I have sent back to them, milord?"

Beads of sweat broke out on the Mayor's lined brow despite the chill of the February day. After a few moments, he spat out, "Tell them they may enter…but just the Yorkist lords. Not their bloody troops. Just the lords. Speak with discretion, though—don't anger them …especially young March. I am thinking soon we won't be calling him by that title anymore…."

Edward rode into the city, flanked by the Earl of Warwick. William Hastings and other great lords. He was the Son of York, the Sun in Splendour, so tall and fair of face men called him the Rose of Rouen. It seemed that light spilt from his form, burning away the drabness of winter, the sombre rule of old King Henry in his food-stained ermine.

He was the Sun, and he brought with him the promise of endless summer and Merry England.

At the same time as he reached London, Margaret of Anjou's army moved—not toward the city but in retreat, hastening toward the Northern holdings of the Lancastrians. For a brief time this retreat would prove a good thing, giving Edward time to plan his next move—but it was in no way surrender on Margaret's part. Once in York, the Queen's army would start to swell in size again as she recruited more men to her cause…and now she had the King at her side to rally the faithful.

Edward decided to move swiftly and decisively. Riding with his lords to Baynard's castle on the side of the Thames, he began to style himself as Edward, the true and just heir of England, France and Ireland. He ignored the Act of Accord, which had bound his father, Duke Richard, to wait until King Henry's death to claim the throne, and spoke of his right by blood through Edward III's third son, Lionel of Clarence, a giant of a man similar in stature to Edward himself. He condemned Henry VI as being of a usurping line, even though the old King had ruled for forty years.

The people of London warmed to this handsome and determined young prince, and in the streets, they began to sing, *"Let us walk within a new vineyard, and let us make a flowery garth, within this month of March, with this fair white rose, this fragrant herb, the Earl of March!"*

Warwick wasted no more time; the uncertainty that had gripped him before St Alban's lifted from mind and body. He sent out word to favourable parties to meet in St John's fields upon Sunday March 1, and then sent his brother Chancellor George Neville, to speak to them of Edward's qualities and nobility.

"And do you wish to be ruled by a feeble man ruled by a foreign Queen?" asked Bishop Neville from a raised platform hastily erected for the occasion.

"No!" the people screamed and shouted, almost as one. (Some of them were Warwick's plants making sure there were plenty of cheers in favour of his protégée.) "We won't be ruled by loons or Frenchwomen! Cast them out of England!"

George Neville cleared his throat, looking very stern, holy and lordly on the high dais. "If it is the wish of the people, would you then accept Edward of March, the son and heir of Richard Duke of York, of royal lineage through Lionel of Clarence, to be your rightful King?"

The crowd exploded into roars and cheers. "Long live King Edward! Long live the Rose of Rouen!"

Grinning with pleasure, Warwick and his entourage hurried back to Baynard's castle where Edward was waiting for news of the outcome of the meeting on St John's Common.

The youthful Duke was standing in the Great Hall, lit with many flambeaux against the early dusk. He was clad in dark blue but of such a hue, in the uncertain light is almost appeared dark purple, royal purple. Beside him stood his mother, Cecily, Dowager Duchess of York, a small but glimmering figure clad in silver and gold tissue, her towering headdress threaded with veils decked out with gemstones. Although her face was still etched with the pain from her recent bereavement, she appeared as regal as the young man by her side—just like a Queen, although she had never worn the crown.

"What is the news, my friend Warwick?" Edward asked gravely as Warwick passed the guards at the door and strode towards him.

The Earl skidded to a halt and dropped to both knees. "By the will of the people, you will be King of England. In plain election, they chose the true son of the blood to rule them from this day forth."

Edward drew a deep breath; his hand clenched as if to take hold of a sceptre…or a sword. "Then so will it be!"

The Duchess of York's eyes gleamed golden with tears that, in her pride, she would not allow to flow freely. "Bring justice back to England," she said softly to her eldest son. "Bring justice to the memory of your father and Edmund." Her lips tightened into a grimace and she raised herself on her toes, to whisper close to his ear, "Grant me my revenge, Edward, I bid you."

He gazed down at her with affection. "So it will be, mother. I am King...but the fight is not yet won, I know that. It is not yet finished. A blood-debt is yet owed."

Several days later, the young King-elect appeared at Paul's Cross, the great preaching pulpit outside the church of St Paul. The Londoners flocked to see him, hailing him as their monarch.

Satisfied, he entered St Paul's where a Mass was said in thanksgiving and celebration. *Laudes Regiae* was sung, as it had not been for any King in over a hundred years, the words ringing out between the pillars of the vast nave:

Christus vincit! Christus regnat! Christus imperat
Exaudi, Christe
Ecclesiae santae Dei salus perpetua
Redemptor mundi, tu illam adiuva
Sancta Maria, tu illam adiuva
Sancta Mater Ecclesiae, tu illam adiuva
Regina Apostolorum, tu illam adiuva
Sancte Michael, Gabriel et Raphael tu illam adiuva
Sancte Ioannes Baptista, tu illam adiuva
Sancte Ioseph, tu illam adiuva
Christus vincit! Christus regnat! Christus imperat!
Exaudi, Christe.

It was the words once chanted to acclaim the Emperor Charlemagne...

Once this was done, bareheaded and magnificent, robed in cloth of gold, Edward rode with his retinue to Westminster, where he sat upon the marble King's Bench as Edward, fourth of that name. Shortly after, he rose and continued in stately splendour to the Abbey, where he seated himself upon the throne and took into his hand the sceptre of St Edward.

However, when the oil of anointing and the crown were brought forward, he raised a hand in protest, to the shock of those present. "I am acclaimed King," he told the delegation of lords and bishops, "but another also claims that title. Not until all my enemies are defeated and my throne is secure shall I wear any crown."

Leaving Westminster Abbey, the crowds were ten deep, the shouts of acclamation both deafening and heartening to the young King. The people had proclaimed him their monarch, favouring him over feeble Henry VI...Now in the days that followed, it would be seen if God Almighty would do the same, the ultimate judge in the war for the throne of England.

Chapter 7

The great Yorkist army began its journey to the north, gaining new recruits as it passed by town and village, swelling like a river in winter when the rains have fallen. The banners flew, bright against the pallor of a sky that threatened a dusting of snow—Edward's new Sunne in Splendour, the Black Bull of his royal ancestor Lionel of Clarence, and the Falcon and Fetterlock of the House of York. Lord Fauconberg's division marched in front, filled with Kentish and Welsh foot soldiers. Sir William Herbert, Walter Blount, Humphrey Stafford and John Howard joined the new King, as did Scrope of Bolton, Viscount Bourchier, Grey of Ruthin, and Lord Fitzwalter. John Mowbray, Duke of Norfolk was unwell with an unknown malady, but he promised to join Edward as soon as he might, bringing a large contingent with him.

Riding next to the King on his caparisoned destrier, Will Hastings stared out across the heaving sea of marching foot soldiers and frowned a little. "The men look hungry, Ned."

"*I* am hungry," said Edward, with a little laugh. "It is Lent, my friend. We are all hungry."

"But will the men have stomachs to fight if their bellies are empty?" Will mused.

Edward's lips curved upwards. "I have thought of this, Will, fear not, and have conferred with my chaplain. The men will be absolved of any sin if there is not enough fish to assuage their hunger. They may eat meat as they please. My wagon trains groan under supplies for the road; I prepared well for the long journey ahead with all the food we need. I have been reading Vegetius."

"Ah, yes, the Roman!"

"Who better than one of those former masters of war? Vegetius wrote that food supplies should always be sufficient for one's army since armies are conquered by starvation as often as the sword. Hunger stabs more fiercely than any blade."

"Wise words, indeed," Hastings nodded. "To tell the truth, though, I can live well enough on cheese and bread and no meat, but wine now, *that* is what I need."

"There will be wine, Will…after the victory. Plenty of it to celebrate the day."

Hastings scratched his chin, gazing out over the frozen English countryside. A hoar frost clung to trees, whitening stumps and fences and the edges of thatched roofs. "Do you think the Lancastrians have decent supplies, up in the north?"

"We can only hope they do not," replied Edward, "but I suspect their provisions may indeed be low."

"The spies have reported back?"

Edward shook his head. "Not as yet, but why do you think Margaret never laid siege to London, why her men have rampaged through the towns like ravening beasts? She has not managed to feed her host. So we must hurry and come upon them before they obtain new supplies…and new heart. The season and the month may aid us here, but we must be swift as the wind! On to the north, my friend…on to Pontefract!"

Warwick, leading the main, arrived at Ferrybridge, the primary crossing point of the Aire, only a few miles from the glowering walls of Pontefract castle, the mightiest fortress in the north and one of ill repute—the unfortunate Richard II had been starved to death in one of its notorious dungeons.

There was no ferry at Ferrybridge and none had existed for over two hundred years; a graceful, eye-catching bridge with seven piers and a chapel had replaced the original ferry.

It did not look so grand now. The Earl of Warwick frowned as he gazed into the gloom. Someone had slighted the old bridge, burning and dismantling the timber structures upon it and damaging the stonework. Arriving first with the vanguard, William Neville, Lord Fauconberg had sent him messages about the destruction before he moved on to a safer crossing point at Castleford.

"The bridge can still be repaired," Warwick told his captain John Radcliffe, Baron FitzWalter. "If we camp here tonight, I will see that the way is freed for our progress. The King should have arrived at Pontefract Castle by now; I will send a message and if he would supply carpenters and stonemasons to repair the damage."

Within a short time, the tradesmen had arrived and began busily working on the wrecked bridge; by dusk, they had made it safe and reopened a path on the right-hand side, ready for passage. Lord FitzWalter set up his encampment nearby to guard the crossing, but he was unconcerned about any attack, joking and laughing with his men as they prepared the camp for the night. As far as the Yorkists knew, the Lancastrian army was still miles away up the road.

Darkness fell and with it a cloud of light snow, corpse-pale and muffling all sound...

The watchman on the bridge stared out into the swirling white flakes, turned golden by the wavering light of his solitary torch. He heard nothing save the rush of the river and the soft hiss of the snow. Even the tongues of nightbirds and beasts were still, quelled by the turning weather. He blinked sleepily, wishing it was time for his relief to arrive, and he could sit down and warm his feet by the fire.

Rubbing his chilled hands together, he began to whistle, marching up and down the newly repaired struts of the bridge...

And then a shadow came, rising up before him through the eddying snowflakes like a monster emerged from an ancient tale. Dark and threatening, it straddled the walkway on the bridge. He could see no eyes, no features.

"Who goes there?" he shouted, hoping the others on the far end of the bridge would hear—but his voice was whipped away by the rising wind.

The figure stepped towards him, full of menace and intent. He reached for his dagger, but in answer, a sword glowed silver-pale, drawn from the folds of a raven-black cloak. Its sharp edge found his gut, bored deep. With a strangled cry, he fell to his knees before a pair of iron-shod feet. The last sound he heard was a guttural laugh as the sword blade was twisted and he was hurled, dying, into the winter-swollen currents of the river.

Butcher Clifford had come.

Lord FitzWalter awoke in his pavilion to the sounds of panicked shouts. Faintly he could hear the clash of metal; men were fighting with weapons around the periphery of the tents. Anger raged through him. His bloody soldiers! Doubtless, they had drunk a skinful too many and were cracking each other's pates or worse. Well, he would put a stop to any trouble in the ranks!

"My lord...your armour?" His squire, a tousled-headed lad called Robert, gazed blearily up from his rush pallet on the floor.

"No time for that!" growled FitzWalter, yanking on his cloak and grabbing a poleaxe. "I will put a stop to these troublemakers who mar my rest."

Angrily, he thrust open the flap of his tent. Snow flurried. He took one step into the night, when a shape raced out of the gloom, a mace upraised in a mailed fist.

He had no time to deflect the blow; he had no time to scream.

Baron FitzWalter only had time to die…

The squire Robert saw his master fall, head cleft, his brains spraying across the ground beside the tent. Crying out in terror, he leapt from his pallet and sped out into the night, hurtling straight past the armoured warrior who had killed his lord. In the shadows men were fighting hand to hand, FitzWalter's camp fully awoken and responding to the threat at last. Behind them, Lancastrian soldiers were pouring across the bridge, the sound of their armour making a terrifying clatter as they swept into the encampment.

Robert ran as if the devil himself was clawing at his heels—and perhaps he was. Soon he reached Warwick's encampment, which stood a short way from FitzWalter's, shielded by a wall of snow-frosted scrub. All was at relative peace, torches burning, men dicing or cleaning weapons prior to retiring for the night.

A guard with a pike blocked his way. "Where are you going young 'un and at such speed?"

"I must see Lord Warwick!"

"At this hour? No chance! What's your hurry, boy?"

The guard looked down at the shivering lad. Suddenly he noticed the boy's feet were bare, red from the coldness of the ground and sprinkled with mire and blood.

"Hang on, tell me wha…"

"Attacked, we've been attacked!" Young Robert cried, tears bursting from his eyes. "Lord Fitzwalter is dead!"

The guard grabbed the boy, lifting him as if he were light as a feather. Realising something was amiss, his colleagues began to sound an alarum; in the clustered tents, more torches flickered to life and anxious voices rang out into the gloom.

Robert was carried to the grandest pavilion of all, that belonging to Richard Neville, Earl of Warwick, emblazoned with the image of the Bear and Ragged Staff and painted robin's egg blue for the Virgin Mary. Thrust through the doorway, the young squire entered the presence of the Earl, who was up, if dressed in a rather slipshod fashion, his squires running madly around him to complete his attire. Both his hair and his eyes were wild.

"What is it, boy? What tidings do you bring?" he shouted, his harsh voice making Robert jump in fright.

Robert sank down into a huddled heap on the floor. "We are undone, my lord...the Lancastrians have attacked us over the bridge. My master, Baron FitzWalter, is slain."

"What? Fitzwalter's dead?" A look of confusion and dismay crossed Warwick's face. "Are you sure?"

"Yes, milord. He never got to utter one word before he was struck down. I saw it with my own eyes! There are hordes of them, all heavily armed...As I fled, I spotted the device of the Lord Clifford."

"Christ! The scouts have failed us utterly...or are dead." Warwick ran his hand through his hair in an agitated motion. I must seek out the King at once."

Pushing Robert aside, the Earl bellowed for his horse and ripped open the flaps of his pavilion, letting in a skirl of frigid wind that nearly killed the fire.

The beast was brought, and a few minutes later, the Earl galloped like a madman into the frigid night, leaving his young squires gaping after him. Young Robert squatted on the floor, massaging his frozen, bloodied feet, and began to weep.

By the time the Earl found his way to Pontefract, King Edward had been roused from slumber by one of his own couriers and was ready in harness. Warwick was surprised how quickly the young man had responded to the evil news. A slight sense of embarrassment curled in his belly as he thought of how he had ridden from camp with scarcely a thought for the men left there.

He pushed aside the thought of a new failure to supplant St Alban's and throwing himself from his lathered steed, fell down before Edward, crying, "It was deepest treachery, Your Grace; they crept upon us like craven dogs seeking fresh meat. My Lord King, I pray God have mercy on their souls, and I leave the vengeance unto God, our Redeemer!"

Then, he drew his sword with a great flash and slit his horse's throat; struggling it went down in a haze of blood. It lay near the surprised young King, blood bubbles puffing softly from the still-twitching nose.

Edward raised his brows and looked sternly at his mentor, Warwick. "Dick?"

The Earl lifted his sword and kissed the jewelled cross-hilt. "I do this deed to show I will not take one step more away from our enemies. Let him fly that will! I will tarry with whoever is brave enough to tarry with me!"

"Then we must fare to the bridge at once!" said Edward. "As it stands, your division fights rudderless."

Warwick's cheeks flared with colour but he raised his blade, still red and dripping with the blood of his stallion. "To the bridge, my King! To the bridge!"

The night was dark, so Edward had many flambeaux lit. Nearing Ferrybridge, the sound of heavy fighting filled the air—screams, shouts, the clash of metal upon metal. Many Lancastrians clustered on the far side of the bridge, dim shapes racing through the gloom, while the Yorkists tried to force them back over the masonry span, hampered by the sections of the bridge still in need of repair. Bodies tumbled into the river's swell, bobbing briefly on the rapids before they were sucked under.

Eager to lead, as he had not done at the time of the first attack, Warwick plunged forward bearing a great battle-axe, fighting shoulder to shoulder with the common man.

But not for long. The Lancastrian force called upon their archers to shoot. The deadly hiss of arrows in flight pierced the shadows, and more Yorkists fell on both bridge span and shore. Warwick suddenly screamed and clutched his leg; a white-fletched bodkin had pierced his armour and wounded him in the thigh. He stumbled and almost fell.

Edward grabbed his shoulder, supporting his friend and mentor. "To me! " he roared at the top of his voice. "Get the Lord Warwick to the surgeon's tent at once!"

Men rushed forward, catching up the slumping Warwick and bearing him away out of harm's way, although he thrashed and hit out at them, crying that he had sworn to fight on.

Edward did not hesitate. Despite the wounding of his kinsman, he did not falter. Immediately he decided that a frontal assault in these circumstances would prove useless. In haste, he sent a summons to Lord Fauconberg and Walter Blount to take their men and cross downriver near their camp at Castleford. If they could ford the river, they would have access to John Clifford's flank.

Fauconberg was a grizzled old warrior, a small, lean man twisted and tough as an old tree root. He was undoubtedly the most experienced soldier amongst the Yorkists, having won his spurs at the Siege of Orleans and taking part in numerous conflicts since. Once a Lancastrian, he had gravitated to Richard Duke of York's cause and was a close relative of both Warwick and Edward through his parents Ralph Neville, First Earl of Westmorland, and Joan Beaufort, daughter of John of G\aunt and Katherine Swynford.

Almost savouring the challenge of battle, the little man thundered along the riverbank on his mount till he found a suitable crossing place for his contingent. The Yorkists pressed on across the cold Aire, their ardour for vengeance heating their blood and making them ignore the icy bite of the waters.

Fauconberg, approaching stealthily through the wintry darkness, flung himself at the side of Clifford's unsuspecting soldiers who were still assailing the bridge. Taken unaware, the Lancastrian flank began to crumble and then was overwhelmed.

A hulking figure wearing armour black as midnight, John Clifford whirled around and sprang astride a waiting steed. "Retreat! Retreat!" he screamed above the commotion of battle, his voice hoarse and thick with unbridled fury.

The Lancastrian force began to pull back, away from the slighted bridge. The Yorkist forces, both those attacking their flank and those still fighting on the span of the bridge, began to roar and push forward in earnest, their spirits soaring as their enemy broke ranks and began to flee.

Old Fauconberg brandished his sword above his head, rallying the levies. "Forward!" he shouted. "Let us hunt these dogs down! Sniff them out and kill the lot!"

The Lancastrian force had now been ripped apart. Men ran wildly along the riverbank, back towards the north, through a whitened haze of scrub and white-swathed trees. Sensing the tide turned in their favour, the Yorkists pounded after them, relentless, their archers picking off the fleeing men with arrows.

William Neville, enjoying the chase, laughed into the wind as he saw John Clifford's small contingent of chosen men riding madly towards the ridge of Dintingdale, east of the village of Saxton. "Butcher Clifford calls his men 'the Flower of Craven!'" he cackled through teeth broken from the time he had been imprisoned by a lowly archer in France. Refusing to surrender, he had nearly died at his captor's hands—but ended up losing his teeth instead of his life when the man punched him into unconsciousness. "Well, tonight the men of York have turned them craven indeed! See how they flee!"

He crooked his hand, gesturing for part of his contingent to strike out across the darkness-shrouded moor. "You will cross the moor and cut the bastards off. The rest of us will ride up behind them. Make sure none escape. None."

Clifford rode like a demon; his horse's hooves struck the frozen earth and made a drumming to match the adrenaline-fuelled thudding of his heart. He knew the main body of the Lancastrian army was not far away—why had he seen or heard nothing from his fellows? Surely, they would be on the march, ready to assist him after his valiant, single-handed attack at Ferrybridge.

Inside his claustrophobic helmet, he scowled. Too many rivalries, too many hatreds amongst the lords of the land. He was not a popular man in any quarter. Those curs who scorned him were not coming to his aid; he knew they were not, God damn them to hell!

Filled with fury, he spurred his steed onwards. Mud and ice splashed up to stain his mount's flanks. On the ridge, where the old Roman road shot straight as an arrow across the landscape, trees stuck up in the dark like twisted black skeletons, waving bony arms in the vicious wind.

Clifford was not a superstitious man, but he was beginning to feel unnerved. At night the landscape was unfamiliar, unfriendly, sinister. He knew the Yorkists were not far behind him, but he could not see their horses; it was easier to deal with an enemy you could see.

Despite his best efforts, he began thinking of his wife Margaret, at home in their castle of Skipton with his three children, Henry, Richard and Elizabeth, all so young, so helpless....

Fool he chided himself, lashing his mount onwards. *What weakness assails me to think womanish thoughts of fire and family? I am doing a man's work...my duty to the King, to the young Prince of Wales who should be his father's rightful heir!*

Suddenly his mount stumbled, throwing a shoe, lame and limping. An oath on his lips, he dismounted and reached to his throat to loosen his gorget and remove his helm...

At that precise moment, a host of riders in enemy colours rent the shadows apart. He opened his mouth to shout to his captain, but no voice ever emerged.

A Yorkist arrow whistled through the darkness and pierced deep into his exposed throat.

Making a horrible gurgling sound, he thudded to the ground. Weakly he clawed at the shaft protruding from his neck; his hands, numb and useless, fell away dripping crimson. Dripping his life's blood …

As light and sentience faded from John Clifford's eyes, his failing brain brought back one final, awful, unwanted memory—the way his hands had dripped red, just as they did now, when he had murdered Edmund of Rutland at Wakefield.

Uttering one final choking groan, he fell on his face, pushing the arrow straight through his neck.

Fauconberg and the Yorkists soldiers descended on the Flower of Craven and slaughtered them to a man.

Edward of York stood over the body of John Clifford. Clifford the Butcher, who had cut off his father's head to gloat upon and had stabbed his brother to death on Wakefield Bridge despite his surrender.

The dead man glared sightlessly up at him, blue-faced and snarling, bloodied lips curled back like those of an animal. His gore-streaked hands were gnarled into claws, clutching at the sky.

"So…Clifford has fallen," said Edward impassively.

"All his men died," said little Lord Fauconberg, flush with victory. "Not one of the Flower of Craven still lives." He gestured with his arm to dark humps spread across the landscape—dead men, dead horses.

Edward nudged Clifford with his foot. Frost was forming on the rigid eyelids, the staring eyes. "This one will not be sent back to his family," he said in a flat voice. "He will go into a pit with the rest of his rabble; may they linger long in Purgatory—or worse. But we will not deal with slain enemies tonight. The greater Lancastrian army must be near and soon we will have to give battle in earnest."

He turned away from the corpse, the arrow still jutting from the torn throat, the black fletchings fluttering in the wind.

"Tomorrow will be the day, my friends. Tomorrow is Palm Sunday."

Chapter 8

The day dawned but sluggishly, a flash of sullen red on the horizon. The unseasonably cold March persisted, with more flutters of snow between patches of tentative sunlight.

The leaders of the Yorkist faction gazed out over Towton Dale, and there was many a heart, no matter how brave, that quailed in its owner's breast—for the view was a terrifying one. Facing the dale were several low hills and on the northernmost, the Lancastrian army gathered, milling like ants as they prepared to do battle. The calls of their trumpets rang across the valley, hard blasts of sound in the frigid air.

The enemy forces were moving, taking their appointed positions, rolling forward like a great dark tide, punctuated only by the coloured of their flaring banners. It was clear now that the Yorkist army was terribly outnumbered by their opponents—and the Duke of Norfolk's men had not yet arrived on the field, being delayed by the distance and by John Mowbray's ill health.

Edward peered out at the masses of men in the distance. Snow was starting to fall in earnest again, blowing wildly on a strengthening northern wind that bit into the bones.

Wiping the obstructive flakes from his eyes, he summoned a messenger to him. "Go find Norfolk; he must not be far behind us now. Tell him to abandon his wains and if he cannot lead himself, hand command over to John Howard—then make haste to join us at Towton Dale. There must be no further delay. Tell him he must not fail me."

The messenger cantered away, and taking a deep breath Edward sprang from his own steed and, removing his helmet, walked out before the banners so that the entire army could see his magnificence. Drawing his sword, he rallied his men as best he could—"Today, if God wills, we will be victorious over our enemies. I will stand with you, to live or to die, as our Saviour and Creator sees fit. Who will stand with me, this Palm Sunday, for St George and for England?"

The army roared its assent, the sound rolling out across the valley to reach the ears of their foes.

And at that same moment, the Lancastrian front began to move, making a great noise of its own with trumpets and drums. The banners of Somerset, quartered with the Arms of England and France, and

Northumberland with his blue lion and red pike flapped madly in the wind.

Fauconberg cast his eyes to the threatening sky; felt the gale strike the back of his helmet almost like an enemy blow. He had fought in such weather conditions before; the incoming storm could well be their opponents' undoing…Quickly, he raised his arm, gesturing to his contingent of archers. "Loose!" he shouted, over the howl of the wind. "Loose now!"

Immediately the air filled with flying arrows. The wind was striking the archers' backs and driving the arrows forward at an even greater speed, slamming them into the Lancastrian line. The opposing archers attempted to return the volley, but the wind sent their shots awry, while the unseasonal snow, growing blizzard-like in intensity, whipped into their faces, hampering vision and accuracy.

Regardless of the archers' plight, the Lancastrian foot soldiers continued to advance. The ceaseless hail of arrows was causing many casualties in their ranks, so they sought to annihilate the Yorkist bowmen, whose almost empty quivers had facilitated a race to collect enemy shafts that had fallen short of the mark.

The Yorkist archers grabbed what they could and turned to flee back to the relative safety of their line. However, they did not take every shaft—instead, they left a small forest of upright arrows bristling from the hard ground to impede their opponents' progress.

Still the Lancastrians ploughed on, facing into the snowstorm. As the Yorkists readied to take them on, bills and poleaxes bristling, out of nearby Castle Hill Woods galloped a group of Lancastrian cavalrymen who had hidden in the dark cluster of trees on orders of Henry, Duke of Somerset. Violently they crashed into the Yorkist left wing, hammering them with axes, swords and war-hammers. The line wavered as men were crushed together unable to use their weapons. Yorkist soldiers began to flee, with the Lancastrians hewing at their heels. Blood now mingled with churned earth; men slipped and fell, their leather boots unable to gain purchase on the unstable ground.

From his position, Edward saw the line waver and the first terrified deserters race out amidst the bloodied bodies that had begun to litter the field. He had to act, or all would be lost!

Charging forward, his standard-bearer at his back, he cast himself manfully into the fray, uncaring of the weather or his own safety. Using his great strength and the advantage of his height, he struck into the Lancastrian hordes, carving out a circle of death around him. Bodies fell, crushed underfoot; screams rang out as limbs were hacked and mutilated. Heartened by their leader's valour, the Yorkists nearest Edward surged forward to guard their lord; cries of agony mingled with the wind's screech as bills and swords pierced armour.

But the Yorkist line held and reformed as best it could, beating back Somerset's cavalry with Edward, uncrowned King, at the forefront, a giant warrior like some hero from the legends of King Arthur, swinging a battleaxe that showered crimson ribbons into the stormy sky.

However, despite the new King's courage, the sheer numbers of the Lancastrian host was gradually pushing the Yorkists forces back. Once again, their line was in danger of breaking…but Edward held firm. "Men, hold!" he roared. "God will guide our hands. The people of England will one day speak of the blessedness of this Palm Sunday Field when York won the day!"

Hearing their lord speak with confidence heartened the Yorkist soldiers and they joined in renewed struggle with their foes, waves of men tangled together in a fight to the death, slipping and struggling, heaving and hewing in a sea of mud and dead bodies. And on blew the incessant, unseasonal snow, hampering vision and adding to the misery of war and death.

For many hours, the two sides grappled with each other, neither gaining the upper hand. Piles of the slain began to line the fields. The snow was blood-soaked, the earth saturated with gore. The Lancastrians still had the advantage of numbers, however, and the Yorkists knew their chances were growing ever more slender as the dreadful day stretched on.

Edward paused in the middle of the killing and hastily moved back behind his archers in order to raise his visor and take a long, cool draught of ale from a flask. He heaved in long breaths of air, then bit back coughing, for even the air bore the bitter iron tang of spilt blood.

Will Hastings suddenly fought his way through the press of the throng, as equally blood-coated as his companion. "Careful, Ned," he said to the young King. "With your visor up, you are at great risk. News has come Lord Dacre has fallen while doing exactly that. A crossbowman took him out while he rested near a tree."

"I must drink, for Christ's sake, Will, lest I faint," said Edward, wiping his mouth as best he could. "And, by God, you lecture me, but have your own visor up to speak to me! Good news about Dacre, though. Once the Lancastrians start losing captains, their soldiers' morale should fail!"

Hastings grinned, though his face was pale and strained. "We will have to pray so, eh, Ned? And if we do not prevail, and we must die, I wish that we should be buried side-by-side facing east and go to heaven or hell together, friends in death as in life. Now get your bloody visor down, goddamn you! You are so great in height you make a perfect target."

Edward laughed and shook his great head, but after throwing down one more mouthful of ale, did as Will Hastings bade and slammed his visor safely shut.

Then it was back into the fray, the mire, the murk and the madness of this most terrible battle for the crown.

Light began gradually to leach from the sky, though few men on the field at Towton even glanced towards the sky, so intent were they on keeping their own lives—and dealing death. Besides, the whole field was obscured—not only by the incessant snow but the strong-smelling smoke from the hand gonnes, which periodically blasted out across the plateau, alarming and dangerous (though mostly to their owners, who were frequently slain as the metal piping ruptured.)

Once again, the Yorkist position began to slip, their ranks pushed backwards by the superior numbers of the Queen's army.

Panting, desperate, Edward glanced over his shoulder as best he could within the confines of his helmet. Where, by Christ, was Norfolk? He had commanded that Mowbray make all haste to the field and yet he still was not here. Surely, he had not turned his coat? Although the Duke was suffering ill health, John Howard, his cousin, was there to take command; Howard was experienced and had always seemed unquestioningly loyal...

Suddenly a trumpet shouted out a fanfare on the far side of the snowbound plateau. Edward craned stiffly around, straining to see through the slim gap in his visor. Far to the side of the field, almost obscured by the press of straining bodies and upraised pikes, half-furled by sleety snow and the smoke discharged by the hand gonnes, was a raised banner that flapped madly in the wind.

It was the White Lion of Norfolk.

The Duke of Norfolk's contingent had overshot the battling armies and come in to throw their fresh might onto the Lancastrian flank.

The course of the battle began to turn. Norfolk's newcomers thrust deep into the enemy line, causing it to waver and then shatter. Mowbray's men under John Howard piled into the midst of their foes, fresh to the fight and eager for battle.

Some of the Lancastrian foot soldiers began to panic and pulling back from the bloody melee began to flee across the bloody field. Others charged the Yorkists with desperate fury. They were beaten back, overwhelmed, slain in their tracks.

From that moment on, for Queen Margaret's army the day was lost. And as more and more men began to run for their lives, heading for the Great North Road, they knew it. It was flight or certain death.

For most, it was bloody ruin either way.

Smelling victory beyond all hope, the Yorkist soldiers responded with an abrupt surge forward. They began to chase their quarry across the field, rage and battle-fury consuming them. By Cock Beck, they caught the Lancastrians trying to ford the stream; so many men piled atop the scanty bridge crossing the water, it let out an almost unearthly groan as the wooden arches collapsed, hurling screaming soldiers into the stream below. They stumbled and grappled, seeking to gain secure footing, trampling their own fellows to death, drowning them as they climbed over the fallen…and then the Yorkists caught up with them.

Many of the Lancastrians had hurled away their helmets to lighten their flight. The Yorkists struck remorselessly at them with poleaxes and bills, even using the hilts of their swords as bludgeons. Skulls were broken open; men's faces slashed asunder and mutilated by rondel daggers and sword blades. Heaps of corpses piled up in the brook, colouring the ice-filled water crimson.

And still, the battle-mad victors continued their violent assault, stabbing and punching and slashing, bringing down men from fifteen to fifty years or more, uncaring of pleas for mercy, uncaring of anything but assuaging the red rage that came with hand to hand combat.

From then onwards, the area near Cock Beck was known as Bloody Meadow….

While the slaughter was taking place at the stream, other fleeing men reached the Great North Road. No solace, no succour did they find, however, as York cavalrymen dashed after them on swift horses, riding them down, stabbing them through the back, striking heads now unprotected with mace and axe and blade. Bodies lay strewn across the road and for several miles on either side.

The Lancastrian army was done. Most of the commanders, their mounts brought by their squires, slipped away into the gloom. Henry Beaufort, along with Exeter and a gravely wounded Northumberland, found their way to the city of York. The Flying Earl James Butler, who had taken ship after Mortimer's Cross to join the northern forces, did not even make it to the field but headed toward Cockermouth to seek another ship into exile.

On the field of death and red ruin Edward stood alone, the Sun in Splendour, a huge figure wreathed in a haze of snow and blood, his banner with the Arms of England emblazoned upon it blown straight out in the gale, a sign for all men to see.

Here stood the true King of England, holding the throne by right of both blood and conquest.

Suddenly he saw something on the ground; he bent to pick it up. A ring fallen from the finger of a wounded or dead Lancastrian, a man of high status for it was gold. He turned it over in his gauntleted hand, seeing a lion crest and the words graven upon it—*NOW YS THUS.*

The wording seemed apt.

Smiling grimly, he flicked the ring away into the mud and snow, to be found by looters of lost for centuries…

There was little fighting taking place now, just aimless killing of the unfortunate remaining Lancastrian foot soldiers and archers, many of whom were already fallen, riddled with wounds. Screams pierced the growing gloom as they were hacked to death or given a swift thrust to throat or eye with a misericorde dagger; already beasts of prey, attracted by the scent of blood, prowled around the edge of the battlefield. Men were stalking between the piles of slain, heaving bodies over and stripping off any useable armour, appropriating weapons, yanking rings from stiff fingers and pendants from slashed necks.

Warwick limped up to Edward, grimacing with every step. The arrow wound he'd taken at Ferrybridge pained him greatly, but it had not stopped him from being in the thick of the battle. "So it is done…your Grace, my King." He swiftly knelt and kissed Edward's hand.

"It is." Edward removed his helm, running his fingers through tousled, sweat-darkened hair, "What news of any deaths of note?"

"Dacre. Welles. And Trollope…along with his son David."

"Andrew Trollope." Edward spat the name. "A traitor to my father at Ludford Bridge and many say the one who devised the plan to bring him to ruin at Wakefield. I do not regret his death…but wish that he had lived so that I could mete out justice to him."

Warwick nodded. "His treachery brought death to my father Salisbury also, captured by then beheaded by Exeter's half-brother the next day…but Trollope will trouble us no more. Let the crows have him! It is more than he deserves."

A muscle twitched in Edward's jaw. "The other lords…Somerset…I assume they have left the field."

"Headed to York, where the false King, his wife and the brat born of cuckoldry, are waiting."

"We will follow them," said Edward grimly, his lips drawn up in a smile that was in no wise pleasant. "Show them what a true King is, shall we not? But first, what prisoners have been taken?"

"Over forty Lancastrian knights, that was the tally," replied the Earl with satisfaction.

"Excellent. They shall receive swift trials here on the battlefield and if their guilt is evident…"

"Which it will be," smirked Warwick, folding his arms over his armoured chest.

"…they will all be executed. God have mercy on their souls, for I shall not have mercy upon their bodies."

Chapter 9

King Edward rode into York arriving in the manner of all royalty through Micklegate with its huge, imposing tower. Gazing upwards, he could see three heads on spikes far above, dark blobs against the clouds. Birds still wheeled, screaming, around them, tearing off the remaining scraps of skin and hair.

Despite their desiccated and battered condition, Edward recognised them instantly—his kinsman Salisbury, his father the Duke and his dear brother Edmund. Openly he began to weep as he had not done in the immediate aftermath of their deaths.

"Have them taken down at once!" he ordered his servants. "Have them placed safely in wooden boxes and taken to the resting places of my kinsmen's bodies in the Dominican priory at Pontefract."

The heads were swiftly removed before the silent crowds of locals, who were shocked by Edward's victory and unsure of him—the people of York had for the most part been loyal to the House of Lancaster. The heads of Lancastrian knights took the place of Edward's kin above the great gateway; the rooks and crows cawed in utter delight and fell upon them in a cloud of black wings, relishing fresh food.

Before the heads of the Duke and Edmund were taken away, Edward went to the men that held the boxes in readiness for transportation to Pontefract. He gestured for them to be opened, and with tears still falling upon his cheeks, stared down at the ruined faces of his father and brother.

"You should have been King," he said to his father's skull, and to Edmund, "and you should have been my loyal brother and advisor all the long years of our lives. But it was not to be. However, God willed that I should avenge you, and now the crown of England is mine and our family claim upheld. And so you shall both lie in peace."

So say, he gestured that the boxes be closed again, and the grim contents were carried from York on their journey to Pontefract. Then Edward passed into the city, as the sun came out and the day brightened. Gradually the sombre mood fallen seemed to change and a few men cheered and several women blew kisses before turning shyly away. Despite their old loyalties, long held, this new King was young and beautiful, and suddenly it seemed as if perhaps he *was* the answer to Harry Six's shambolic rule. A new day had dawned over England; out with the oppressive old, in with the new.

Edward took lodgings in one of York's many religious houses and sent out spies to hunt down any Lancastrian lords hiding in the city. In the afternoon, he called his faithful to a council and told them of what he had learnt.

"The false King and his family have fled toward Scotland," he announced. "They are far ahead on the road; they must have left shortly after the battle began, so near to the border are they."

"Is it worth pursuing them?" asked Warwick, easing himself into a chair, mindful of his wounded leg. "I am ready if it's your wish…blast this bloody leg!"

"We will go and show them that my power is not to be threatened…but I doubt we will catch them—our men are too tired and battle sore. The further north Margaret and Henry go, the more protection they will have from their supporters; the far north is their territory, as you know even better than I, Dick, for many of your holdings lie in the north. And to pursue them over the Scottish border—utter madness. But we will make them know that even in their own heartlands of support, they are done."

Warwick glowered, still wincing with the pain in his leg. "So…we most likely cannot catch them. That means they will still wait in readiness, eager to torment all good Englishmen in time and thrust their puppet back on the throne."

"Let them wait. I have destroyed their army. I am acclaimed King and soon will be crowned King. All men surely must now see Henry's unworthiness; he is no warrior. So who would they follow in renewed war—the harridan Margaret? The child of dubious ancestry?"

"That child will grow to be a man." One of the lords, Walter Devereux, shook his head darkly. "Do not forget that, your Grace. He will not remain a child for long."

"And when he does grow to man's estate, let him come at me then, if he has the stomach for it. The result then will be no different to now."

Edward stalked around the room; the fire was roaring on the hearth, its light striking the rubies on his fingers and on his collar of Suns and Roses with the gleaming golden pendant of the Lion of March hanging down. "There is better news too, my lords. Northumberland is dead; he reached York but died of wounds taken in the battle. Thomas Courtenay, the Earl of Devon has been captured—he could not escape the town because illness fell laid him low…Wretched he is now, writhing with gut pain while in chains, but he will be far more wretched when he has no head!" He grinned; the firelight cast stretching shadows over his young face, making him seem older, sterner, a King wreathed in bloody light. "But even better, to my ears, are the tidings from Cockermouth. James Butler is in custody there, along with Queen Margaret's clerks John Morton and Ralph Mackerell."

"Doctor Morton." Will Hastings' eyes narrowed. "Always an oily sort and he and Margaret were thick as thieves. I know what you plan for Butler, but what about the two churchmen? A different dilemma, eh, Ned?"

Edward tapped his fingers on the table, thinking. "I will not execute men of God. Although sometimes I deem it better to be feared than loved, I do not want to start my rule with such bloodshed and have the people turn from me. I think I might...pardon them."

"Pardon!" Warwick yelped, leaping up then clutching his leg in agony. "Those loyal Lancastrians?"

Edward nodded. "A man like Morton is most loyal to his paymaster, I'd warrant. We will see." He moved to the door, gleaming like an earth-bound sun, the torchlight making a halo of his newly washed and combed hair. He looked more courtier now than warrior-king, but muscles ripples beneath the tightness of his ornate doublet. "But first, I must prepare for Courtney's execution...and see that his head is set above Micklegate where my father's head once was displayed."

The subsequent day in York wAS filled with much joy. Not only were the Lancastrian forces dispersed and Northumberland dead, but the Yorkists had found John Neville, Lord Montagu, and John Bourchier, Lord Berners, alive and well. Captured at St Alban's, they had been dragged across the country at high status prisoners, their lives in danger at every minute but when it had come to it, the Lancastrians had left them unharmed. They had been confined in a deep, dark dungeon beneath York Castle, filled with rats and creeping water, but, at the last, as the Lancastrians fled, were set free by the local gaolers. Although they were unkempt and in need of a bath and a shave, they were both unharmed.

Warwick clapped his younger brother on the shoulder in joy. "I thought I would not see you again, John. Praise Our Lord and Saviour that your captors spared your life. It would go hard to lose another brother, as well as a father, to the Lancastrian axe."

John held out his hands while servants bound cuts and scrapes on his fingers and arms; others brought an ewer and laved his face with fine linen cloths. "At times I despaired of ever seeing the sun again, but I thought on how I had previously survived imprisonment with our brother Thomas at Chester and so strove to keep up my hopes. I do not know why, in the end, they spared me."

"I do," said Richard Neville with a throaty chuckle. "Remember that I hold Somerset's brother in Calais. If you were harmed in any way..." He made a slashing motion across his throat. "Also the Mayor of York prevailed upon the Lancastrian lords that you should be spared."

"Did he? Kindness or something else?"

"Something else. He knew that if you and Bourchier were executed, Edward would sack York in revenge. He certainly didn't want that to happen."

"No, I would think he did not, hearing of the destruction to diverse towns by those miscreants loyal to Margaret of Anjou. He must have known well what damage Edward could wreak."

"So...how many perished at Towton, Dick?" Montagu looked over at his brother with interest. "I have heard the Lancastrians suffered such losses they will never be able to raise a full-sized army again unless they recruit Scots or the French."

Warwick slowly paced the room. "The heralds have come to a tally, but I know not how much truth there is in it...Edward's army is said to have lost 8000 men."

Montagu's eyes widened and his face paled. "Jesu Christ! 8000! I marvel that you and the King still live and breathe upon the earth with losses so great."

Warwick's lip twisted upwards. "Ah, but, John...the heralds' tally for Lancaster is far higher. They say that 20,000 died."

John Neville was stunned into silence at the enormity of the number of slain; the servants diligently went on dabbing him with cloths and water while squires ran about dressing him in clean, decent clothes.

At length, he found his tongue. "Twenty...twenty..."

"So they say. Enough that they formed a bridge of bodies when the wooden bridge over Cock Beck collapsed."

Montagu grimaced at the thought, even though his brother spoke of enemy soldiers. "And where will they be entombed, all those dead men? The churchyards will be full for miles about!"

"Most of them will not be buried, not a proper Christian burial anyway." Warwick's voice was harsh. "For our own, we will do what we can, God rest their souls. The enemies…let them be thrown into large pits. Most of them are unrecognisable anyway…or soon will be; the scavengers were already on the field when we pursued the remnant of Margaret's army, and not all of them walked on four legs or came on wings."

Montagu crossed himself, looking down at the floor; the Lancastrians were foes but still men, and as they would not receive a Christian interment, they would be doomed to a long spell in purgatory.

Noting his brother's expression, the Earl of Warwick sniffed haughtily. "They backed the wrong man. The wrong King."

"Ah, yes, our bright young King. We will be heading south for Edward's coronation soon, I take it?"

Warwick shook his head. "Not yet, Edward still has business in the north. As do we. I fear that once Edward turns south, we must needs stay in the area to help keep the peace. The castles of Bamburgh, Dunstanburgh, and Alnwick are still in Lancastrian hands, and they are important fortresses that could be used to foment unrest. But let us not think on hard tasks right now! Let us celebrate our great victory…this land is forever changed from this day forward."

Montagu beckoned to the servants to bring wine for him and for his Warwick. He raised his goblet aloft, its contents gleaming red like the blood that had poured upon the snow at Towton.

"To victory, brother. And to you, King-maker and soldier. And to Edward, our new King!"

Chapter 10

Edward stayed in York only long enough to see Courtney of Devon duly executed, along with Baron Rougemont-Grey, who was found hiding in a cellar in the castle. Their heads joined the others on Micklegate Bar. Then the new King took horse and hurried north with a goodly part of his army towards Newcastle, where there were signs of strong resistance by Lancastrian forces.

First, though, he halted at Durham, with its great Norman Abbey and castle high on the banks overlooking the deep, wide river. Bishop Lawrence Booth, once Queen Margaret's chancellor, came to greet the new Monarch, a spare, serious man who approached the new young King with wariness.

"You need not fear me," Edward told him, as he walked through the ornate Norman prior's door of the Abbey, wrought centuries ago to resemble the doors at the Shrine of Santiago de Compostela. "I bring no harm to true, honest men. I know you as a man of talent and would that you bring your piety and holiness to bless my reign. What say you?"

"If God has given you victory and it seems He has, I would be glad to guide you in his goodly ways, Highness." The Bishop inclined his silvered head. "I serve whom God has chosen."

"Excellent," said Edward, throwing the Bishop a winning smile. "As of this day, I shall make you my confessor, my lord Bishop. Let us now look upon the shrine of the blessed St Cuthbert, which lies within this mighty House of God."

So Bishop Lawrence and the King, followed by Lord Warwick and William Hastings, processed down the aisles with their great, rounded Romanesque columns and came upon the shrine of Cuthbert behind a stone screen paid for by Edward's great grandfather, John Neville. Decorated with statuary that included the Virgin Mary flanked by the northern saints Cuthbert and Oswald, it was the prime holy site of northern England. Gems glittered about the shrine and over it stretched a gilded cover adorned with carvings of dragons and other fanciful beasts.

When the King had finished praying at the shrine, kneeling on flagstones worn by generations of pilgrims' knees, he returned to the nave with the Bishop and his two companions.

To his surprise, near the door of the abbey hovered the Prior John Burnaby, wringing his hands like an old woman in distress. Bishop

Lawrence seemed perplexed by his presence. "Prior, what is the meaning of this intrusion? Could it not wait till later?"

"No...no, my lord Bishop," said Prior Burnaby. "I seek to speak with the King on a cause of great import to the abbey."

Edward's brows lifted in surprise at this presumption, but Bishop Lawrence placed his hand upon Prior Burnaby's arm. "You are a good man, Prior, even though your timing is a little...unseemly. I will vouch for you before the King."

Turning, Booth stiffly knelt before Edward. Warwick, who had been trailing behind the King, now also sank down on one knee. "I too can vouch for Prior Burnaby; I have known him long years. I beg that you be a good lord to him."

"Speak then." Edward inclining his head towards the Prior. "Good men I trust have spoken this day of your probity."

"My lord King..." Burnaby nervously licked his lips. "My monks were compelled by the old Queen Margaret to give her 400 marks for her cause. The worst money ever spent, and it hurt us all grievously. We...I...uh...your Grace, we wondered if you could, in your tender mercy, give this sum back to the Abbey."

There was a moment's silence. Hastings bit back a choking laugh. Then Edward flung back his head and his own laughter boomed out, making priests and monks within the abbey church turn to gaze in shocked surprise.

"You paid my enemy to work against me, and now you want me to give it back to you out of my own coffers?" Edward's shoulders shook with unrestrained mirth.

Prior Burnaby flushed to the roots of his cropped hair and stared down at his sandals. "Your Grace, I have given offence...forgive me..."

Edward shook his head and quelled his mirth, quickly becoming serious. "There is nothing to forgive, Prior. I swear to be that which my companions ask me to be—a good and just lord. I will not forget your bill."

Then the King left the great Abbey and its bells pealed out in strident clangour over the town below, and people waiting to see the new ruler celebrated and danced in the streets.

"It is as if they worship him, Bishop," remarked Prior Burnaby, standing beside his superior and watching Edward's progress through the bustling town.

"Perhaps they do," said Bishop Lawrence.

"Is it right, though, that they worship a mortal man in this way?"

Booth glanced at him. "Long I worked for old King and his Queen. I prayed many a night on bended knee that God would heal his anointed who lay sick in his bed, unaware of all around him. God did not respond and evil counsellors held sway. So I can only think God turned his face from Henry and Margaret for some great sin, and He smiled instead on the son of York." He laughed a little to himself. "So, Burnaby, give the people time to worship this bright new hope. Eventually, they will see that he, too, is but a fallen man, flawed and sinful, albeit King. But not now. Not today. It is their day. And his."

King Edward travelled with his retinue to Newcastle, where the city gates and the great black keep were held against them by ardent Lancastrians. The defence was half-hearted, however, and the gates soon fell, with the castle garrison surrendering shortly thereafter.

Edward assumed his position in the keep, and then sent for James Butler and Doctor Morton and Mackerell who were under armed guard at Cockermouth. He received the two Doctors into his presence first, leaving them on their knees for a good long while, as he fastened an unwavering gaze upon them and looked both stern and thoughtful.

"You know I should take both your heads," he said, at length. "You, Morton, I specifically excluded from the pardon I gave upon the 6th of March. Such a harmless creature you look, kneeling there—well fed, like a pigeon, with that fat, smiling face…but I deem you have one of the quickest and most devious minds in the country. You're a dangerous man."

Doctor Mackerell was shivering and shuddering, clearly believing he was to be hauled off to the block at any moment. Morton, however, remained calm and cool despite the King's harsh words. "If my mind is quick, it may be turned to good uses," he said. "I would serve you, your Grace."

"Would you?" Edward glared at him. "Is it not said that a man may not serve two masters?"

"I serve only one master…" Morton rolled his eyes up towards heaven.

"Are you sure that's your true master, though?" Edward mocked. "Maybe you should be looking down below instead. Down towards the demons in the fiery pits that jab the buttocks of treacherous men with pitchforks…"

Morton still showed no fear. "I see the future, your Grace. King Henry is the past; God has made his judgment. I cede to God in all things, and thus I leave Henry of Lancaster to his fate. Jesu help him…" He crossed himself piously. "Henry is no better now than the idiot who rants in the market square or the loon who barks at the moon."

"I will think on your words," said Edward; his voice was cold, indifferent.

"And I will keep my head?"

"You are presumptuous. I am sending you and that quivering fool next to you to the Tower while I make my ultimate decision on your fates."

Mackerell made a mewling noise at the mention of the Tower but Morton bowed low, his robes swishing against the rush-strewn flagstones of Newcastle keep. "Your Grace is kind and merciful…"

"Maybe, maybe not, do not presume…now go!" Edward gestured to the guards arrayed around the castle's Great Hall. "Take these two away and keep them under lock and key—at least one I deem is as slithersome as a serpent. Have them transported to London and confined to the Tower."

The guards led Morton and Mackerell out of the vast chamber and Edward leaned back in his gilded seat beneath a canopy dotted with roses and rayed suns. Next, he would see the man he hated more than almost anyone, the man who was there at his father's death at Wakefield.

James Butler, the Flying Earl.

Butler was brought in, his hands and feet manacled and a gang of armed soldiers around him. His face was the colour of curds, his vibrant blue eyes wide and bright with fear. Black curls were plastered with sweat to his cheeks.

"So…" Edward bent forward, taking in Butler's bedraggled appearance. "The Flying Earl has at last been caught in flight and now must face the consequences of his actions. Have you anything to say for yourself?"

Butler hesitated as emotions rushed over his face, first flickering, unrealistic hope, then fear, then…utter hatred. Then he spat out, "No, I have nothing to say, for I know you would not listen. If this is to be my last day upon this earth, I will not speak so as to be mocked by you, usurper."

Edward rose, stepping in stately fashion to stand next to his prisoner. He towered over him by a head. "They call you a handsome man. At one time it was reputed you were the most handsome man in the realm. Men whispered that your fair face was the reason you fled from every battle—you feared that lovely visage of yours would perish and the ladies of the court reject you. Is this true?"

"It is NOT true," Butler hissed between clenched teeth.

"So…you are just a plain coward then, is that the truth?"

Defiant, Butler spat at the King's feet. "Whatever I am no longer matters. I have but one thing to say—I am glad I fought at Wakefield. I saw your father slain. I saw him dragged upon an anthill before the blow was struck. I saw them put a paper crown upon his wretched head."

A tense muscle twitched in Edward's cheek but he did not respond in fury, refusing to be goaded into rage, to show weakness before the assembled nobles and clergy in the hall.

"You will wish you had flown from Wakefield like all your other battles," Edward said in a voice remarkably calm, even. Then he gestured to Butler's gaolers, waiting impatiently behind him. "Transport this creature to the market square and there see him beheaded him with all speed. The Flying Earl will now fly only to the grave. Then, when the act is done, put that pretty, pretty, arrogant head upon the town gates, no longer fair, but foul. Food for the crows, naught more."

The King stayed in the north for a few more days, dealing with small outbreaks of violence and listening to news about the flight of his foes. Confirmation came that Henry and Margaret had indeed reached the Scottish court, where they were greeted cordially and given refuge.

"I will not linger any longer in the north," Edward told Will Hastings and Warwick. "I have shown at York and at Newcastle that I will not be trifled with. I shall go on a progress so that my subjects can see me. The ordinary man will have heard by now of my prowess upon the field, but I want him to know his King for more than warfare. I want him to know that I will rule him with an even hand, tempering justice with mercy, and listening to his pleas and grievances. You, Warwick, stay here and do what you might for my cause."

So Edward with his retinue travelled down through Lancashire, Cheshire, Staffordshire, Northamptonshire, Buckinghamshire and on to the royal palace of Sheen, where he set his Coronation date for July 12 and prepared for a session of parliament. However, disquieting rumours arose within days—the French were restive and likely to invade; pirates roamed the seas, harming trade with the continent; in the north, the Scots, emboldened by their Lancastrian guests, were pelting over the border and causing mayhem. Margaret of Anjou, currying the favour of the Scottish regent, Mary of Gueldres, magnanimously presented Scotland with the town of Berwick, which stood upon the border—a move deliberately made to rile the new King.

"Christ, Will," said Edward to Hastings, as he sat before a desk already heaped with rolls and parchments—accounts, declarations, pleas, "this will not do. Trouble and more trouble. I must get the crown upon my head as soon as possible, and let our foes know the opportunity to come and take it is not open to them. Now or ever. Let us move the Coronation forward to June 28."

"A wise move," said Hastings. Edward had promised to make him a Baron and moving the Coronation date forward might well benefit his aims. "As always, Ned."

"Now, enough work..." Edward lazily moved his arm across the desk, flinging the less important documents to the floor. "My eyes have grown tired. Shall we go find some pretty ladies to spend a few hours in our company?"

"Yes, my lord King," laughed Hastings, his small, shrewd eyes glittering at the thought. If things continued in this manner, with lots of play as well as work, his friend Edward's reign was going to be glorious indeed.

On June 26 Edward entered the stalwart walls of the city of London. Clad in scarlet, his chain of office shining, the Mayor came to greet him, and surrounded by the Aldermen of London and a crowd of notable residents, he was escorted to the Tower of London, shining white beneath the cloudless summer sky.

Inside the Tower, Edward received a stream of men who had aided him at Ferrybridge and Towton and made them all knights—including dogged, loyal John Howard and William Stanley, brother of the side-changing Lord Thomas Stanley, who seemed a little more firmly for York than Thomas the Trimmer.

When he was done and the room had emptied save for his servants and squires, the King glanced around and frowned. "I think I am missing two of those to be made knights. The youngest, who shall, concurrent with my wishes, be knighted today."

He nodded to the page that stood in the corner, awaiting his master's pleasure. "Bring them to me, Peter. It is time. I am eager to see them again."

The page bowed and vanished. A short while later footsteps rang out in the corridor beyond the King's chamber as two young boys ran down it, almost pushing each other in their excitement to get at the King.

One of the lads had dark golden curls and a plump pink and white face; the other, the younger, was small and thin, his hair wavy and losing its baby fairness. Both were dressed in fine velvet doublets; a sky-blue for the elder and a rich red for the younger. Both wore long-toed imported shoes over which they tripped, not quite used to the great pikes on the end.

"Ned!" squealed the older boy, pushing forward. "You are King! You've avenged father and Edmund! How many of the wicked Queen's men did you kill? Tell me, Ned!"

Suddenly the smaller boy grabbed the other's elbow; the two children crashed together, both skidding on the polished tiles. "George! Wait! Ned...Ned is the King now! You...we...we can't call him 'Ned' anymore. We can't run up to him...he's the KING!"

The two boys disentangled from each other and slid down on their knees before Edward's seat, their heads bowed reverently. "Forgive us, Ne...your Grace. We were noisy and rude," said the smallest boy. "We didn't mean to be."

Edward laughed, and rising, reached forward and ruffled the hair of both lads. "I will forgive you willingly. I confess I am as pleased to see you as you are to see me, George, Richard. I trust your brief stay in Burgundy was not too onerous."

"I was brave!" George Plantagenet puffed himself up with pride. "Since I am now the second eldest male of the House of York, mother said I must be a man...unlike Richard, who is still just a baby."

"I am eight," shot back Richard, eager to refute George's earlier jibe about his age. "I am *not* a baby. A baby would have cried on the ship when it rocked. I was as brave as George. I did not cry."

"I am sure you were *both* brave. Both of you are of the House of York, sons of our late father of blessed memory."

Richard looked a little tearful at the mention of their father, but George's face took on an angry expression. "I would have fought with you, Edward...for our father...and Edmund. I would have."

"You are only eleven, George. Pray that neither you nor Richard shall know such destruction as I have seen. Pray that God, in his mercy, brings England peace at last."

The two little boys were silent, chastened.

"But come…" Edward raised the children to their feet. "Today I will make my beloved brothers knights to serve and protect in the future. For the Coronation, I will make you Duke of Clarence, George, as you are now my heir presumptive. Fear not, Richard, you will not be forgotten; when you are a little older, you shall be Gloucester."

Trying for adult propriety, young Richard dutifully kissed his brother's hand. George just looked Edward in the eye. "Thank you, sir, but you still have not told us…How many Lancastrians did you slay?"

"Thousands!" roared Edward, suddenly laughing. "With one swing of my trusty sword!"

On Sunday, June 28, Edward walked to Westminster Abbey for his Coronation. The sun blazed overhead and women swooned at the sight of their new King, whom they called 'the most handsome prince in Europe.' Rather than keeping the stern face and distant manner of most kings in the past, Edward smiled at the crowds as he reached the porch of the great building and the people loved him for it. Yes, there were a few, skulking in workshops or brewer's yards or taverns who sneered at the 'young upstart', and called him names like 'twatt' and 'tourde', but they were few and far between. Now that mad Henry was gone, the people shook themselves and roused, as if from a long, troubled sleep.

The Sun had risen in Splendour. The Summer King had come.

For to save all of England was the Rose's intent,
With Calais and London and Essex and Kent,
And all Southern England up to the waters of the Trent,
And when he saw the best time, The Rose of Rouen went,
Blessed be the time, that ever god spread that flower!

The way into the North Country, the Rose full fast sought
With him went the Ragged Staff that many men there brought,

So did the White Lion full worthily wrought,
Almighty Jesus, bless his soul that their armies taught.
Blessed be the time, that ever God spread that flower!

Stanzas from the 15th century poem THE ROSE OF ROUEN

AUTHOR'S NOTES—BLOOD OF ROSES is strongly based on the real events of Edward IV's seizure of the throne in 1461. Occasionally, I may have tweaked the time scale slightly (but only very slightly) for flow. A few minor points are debatable; some sources say Edward was in Gloucester for Christmas when he heard of his father's death at Wakefield, others say Shrewsbury. I used Gloucester because I know the town a little better. Also, the field where George Neville stood on a raised dais and preached Edward's merits as king was listed as St George's by two historians and St John's by two others. Reading the history of the two places, I am almost 100% certain it would be St John's. Then there is the matter of the Croft brothers. For years many historians have assumed that Edward and Edmund complained about them in their well-known letter to their father. However, I agree with Dr John Ashdown-Hill that the letter has been misread. They are not complaining about the Croft's behaviours towards themselves but toward the Crofts from someone else in the household. Certainly, the Crofts ended up as strong supporters, especially at Mortimer's Cross.

Towton was the bloodiest battle ever fought on English soil, but it remains one of the lesser-known battles in English history (and Mortimer's Cross is even less known.)

Excavation over ten years has revealed some of the grave pits, and the analysis of the remains revealed a truly terrifying picture of medieval warfare. Of 38 males between the ages of 16-50, all of those whose skulls were recovered had severe cranial trauma. Sharp implements had inflicted nearly three-quarters of these wounds; just over a quarter by blunt trauma and twelve by puncture. Many of them had more than one injury, some easily a dozen.

For many years, the dead combatants had lain in large pits on the battlefield, poorly buried; it was said that huge clouds of gasses hung over the field by night, giving rise to legends of ghosts. Edward never built any memorial to the dead of his great victory, but his younger brother did so—in 1483, Richard III began to build a chapel there and ordered some of the remains moved into consecrated ground. This must have been an awful job for the medieval excavators as osteological reports show that many bones were still articulated, with desiccated tendons and ligaments holding them together. There were a couple of graves that held a lone occupant, laid out in the usual Christian fashion, including an man with an arrow in his thigh—possibly these men were commanders.

Richard's memorial chapel was almost complete when he was killed at Bosworth, and the Tudors quickly let the building fall into ruin, the stones being dragged elsewhere for use.

The chapel was long thought to have been lost forever; however in 2013, remains of the chapel were found including medieval stonework and fragments of leaded glass. The chapel appears to have been subsumed into the fabric of Towton hall, which is why some of the skeletons were found beneath the dining room floor...

If you have enjoyed my story of the WARS OF THE ROSES, please have a look at my other books set in this period.

The I, RICHARD PLANTAGENET series.

Series of 4 books (3 published, one coming out this year) told from the first person viewpoints of the main character, and it told in a slightly lighter, more humorous style than is usual.

I, Richard: Tante le Desiree, is told from Richard Duke of Gloucester's viewpoint from the Battle of Barnet to the Scottish wars in 1482

I, Richard: Loyaulte Me Lie. Richard as King, from his viewpoint. The triumph and the tragedy up to the fatal charge on Bosworth field

A Man Who Would Be King. First person account of one of the dark horses in the Wars of the Roses, Henry Stafford, Duke of Buckingham, blamed in several documents as the killer of the princes. Did Harry want a throne for himself? Did Aunt Margaret, Henry Tudor's mum, interfere?

(A complete edition containing both Tant le Desiree and Loyaulte Me Lie is also available—saves you money!)

SACRED KING. Historical fantasy novella of Richard III's experiences after death and his return in a Leicester carpark

WHITE ROSES, GOLDEN SUNNES. A collection of stories about Richard III and his family

THE FEAST OF THE INNOCENTS-short story about Richard's son Edward of Middleham

Other Books with a Medieval Theme—

MY FAIR LADY-the life of the maligned Queen Eleanor of Provence

MISTRESS OF THE MAZE-The Fair Rosamund, mistress of Henry II

THE CAPTIVE PRINCESS (due out by end of April 2018)-The tragic life of Eleanor of Brittany, kept prisoner almost all her life due to her closeness to the throne.

THE HOOD GAME-Rise of the Greenwood King. Mystical retelling of the Robin Hood legend. Part 2 due out this year.

OTHER—

THE STONEHENGE SAGA COMPLETE. 2 novels about a Bronze Age war lord who becomes master of Stonehenge with the aid of the Merlin, a powerful shaman.

MY NAME IS NOT MIDNIGHT. Dystopian fantasy. A young girl escaped her cruel teacher in a cold, snowy dystopian world and ends up on a quest to free magic

A DANCE THROUGH TIME- Isabella tumbles through the floor in an old theatre…into Victorian times and the arms of brooding Augustus Stannion. Time Slip Romance.

PLEASE FOLLOW ME ON AMAZON!

"

25532463R00042

Printed in Poland
by Amazon Fulfillment
Poland Sp. z o.o., Wrocław